P.S. Barford,
London,
2. iv. 60

THE FABER
POPULAR RECITER

THE FABER
POPULAR RECITER

EDITED BY
KINGSLEY AMIS

FABER AND FABER
LONDON   BOSTON

First published in 1978
by Faber and Faber Limited
3 Queen Square London WC1N 3AU
Reprinted 1979 (twice)
Printed in Great Britain by
Whitstable Litho Ltd., Whitstable, Kent
Introduction and this selection
© 1978, Kingsley Amis

British Library Cataloguing in Publication Data

The Faber popular reciter.
1. Recitations   2. English poetry
I. Amis, Kingsley   II. Title
821'.008   PN4201

ISBN 0-571-11287-0
ISBN 0-571-11339-7 Pbk

CONTENTS

7

8

14

INTRODUCTION

When I was a schoolboy before the Second World War, the majority of the poems in this book were too well known to be worth reprinting. If they were not in one anthology they were in a couple of others; they were learned by heart and recited in class, or performed as turns at grown-up gatherings; they were sung in church or chapel or on other public occasions. Some were set as texts for classical translation, an exercise that gives you an insight hard to achieve by other means: the fact, noted by my fellows and me, that Mrs Hemans's 'Graves of a Household' went into Latin elegiacs with exceptional ease encourages a second look at that superficially superficial piece.

Most of that, together with much else, has gone. I suppose hymns are still sung here and there, classical verses written and – another way of gaining insight – poems learned by heart and recited. But in any real sense the last could only happen at school, as part of an academic discipline. Any adult who commits a poem to memory does so for personal satisfaction; if he utters it in company he does so to share it with like-minded friends (or as a harmless means of showing off), and as one who quotes, not as one who recites.

I should be sorry, then, if readers of this book were to be confined to those in search of material for what we usually understand by recitation. 'Reciter' is a nineteenth-century term used here for a collection of characteristically nineteenth-century objects: poems that sound well and go well when spoken in a declamatory style, a style very far indeed removed from any of those to be found at that (alas!) characteristically twentieth-century occasion, the poetry recital, with all its exhibitionism and sheer bad art. If recitation has died out in the family circle, reading aloud has not, and it is as material for this that my anthology is ideally intended; let me remind the doubtful that here is a third way, less troublesome than the first two, of finding out more about a piece of writing and so enjoying it more. Others will perhaps be glad to have within one binding a number of old favourites now obscured by changes in taste or fashion; yet others, younger than the other others, may make a discovery, if only that poetry need be none the worse for being neither egotistical nor formless.

I mentioned just now the nineteenth century as the main source of my selection, and sure enough a good two-thirds is drawn from authors born either in its course or so soon before as to have done the larger part of their growing-up within it, between 1788 and 1888. More than this, the pieces from longer ago are very much of the sort that the nineteenth-century poetical outlook could accept without strain: Shakespeare at his most direct, Milton on his blindness, ballads, hymns, the patriotic, the sententious (Wotton, Gray). Thus the Elizabethan period and the years immediately following contribute more than the major part of the seventeenth century, and there is one solitary poem in the Augustan heroic couplet.

No age of course has a single poetical outlook, always half a dozen; I was talking about the kind of person of that time who was intelligent and educated without having what we would now call literary tastes, who liked poetry without finding it in any way a necessity and much of whose contact with it would have been through recitation and song, both sacred and profane. What our man, or woman, required is what fits verse for rendering in those ways: absolute clarity, heavy rhythms and noticeable rhymes with some break in the sense preferred at the end of the line. (Outside Shakespeare, understood to be a special case, there are only two blank-verse pieces here, both by Tennyson, a different special case.) Subject-matter must suit the occasion by being public, popular, what unites the individual with some large group of his neighbours. The emotional requirement is that the reader, or hearer, be stirred and inspirited more than illuminated or moved to the gentler emotions: love poetry, for instance, can often be recited effectively, but not in the course of the kind of recitation I have described. For another set of reasons, comic poetry is likewise inappropriate.

The exclusions necessitated by all this obviously exclude a very large part of the best poetry in the language, even of that written in the nineteenth century. For instance, I have felt bound to omit Wordsworth, the poet of Nature: 'The Solitary Reaper' gets in because it takes an untypically detached, almost a towns-man's, view of the central figure. Shelley, Browning and Arnold are among those less than fairly represented; Charles Kingsley, Alfred Austin and Austin Dobson are not greater poets than Coleridge, Keats and (some would add) Hopkins, who are altogether left out. Perhaps popular poetry, outside the accidental contributions of poets whose critical esteem rests on other achievements, can never be anything but what George Orwell called good bad poetry.

The phrase occurs in his entertaining and valuable review-article on Kipling, whose works he describes as 'almost a shameful pleasure, like the taste for cheap sweets that some people secretly carry into middle life'. Orwell goes on to give other examples of good bad poetry, half of which I have included here, and remarks, accurately enough on his terms, that there was no such thing until about 1790. The characteristics of this kind of poetry, he says, are vulgarity and sentimentality, though he softens the latter term by adding: 'A good bad poem is a graceful monument to the obvious. It records in memorable form – for verse is a mnemonic device, among other things – some emotion which nearly every human being can share. The merit of a poem like 'When All the World is Young, Lad' ['Young and Old'] is that, however sentimental it may be, its sentiment is 'true' sentiment in the sense that you are bound to find yourself thinking the thought it expresses sooner or later, and then, if you happen to know the poem, it will come back into your mind and seem better than it did before. Such poems are a kind of rhyming proverb. . . .' Sentiment is usually considered different from and higher than sentimentality, and an example with almost universal appeal (which is perhaps a nice way of saying 'vulgar') hardly seems to deserve being called bad, even good bad. Not all popular verse, again, is in the Kipling manner; perhaps that manner deserves to be called vulgar and sentimental, though to me it does not in principle, but I can find nothing of either quality in, say, 'The Old Squire', '1887', 'Ha'nacker Mill' or the poems of the Great War that close the volume. Indeed, to anyone not blinkered by political prejudice, from which category I would exclude Orwell, 'The Soldier' must surely be counted one of the greatest poems of our century.

And yet . . . Well, I have included 'Horatius' entire; I could not bear to cut so much as a single stanza; even to glance at it in the course of preparing the book sent a thrill through me; it is probably the best and most characteristic example we have of military-patriotic popular verse – in it, Rome of course has the appeal of a golden-age England, though there are English notions in the ranks of Tuscany too. And yet there is something unreal, something almost ritualized about it, not vulgar nor sentimental as those words are normally applied, something not of pretence but of let's-pretend. The brave days of old belong to the time when all the world was young: this is what used to be called a boy's poem, founded on values that are few, simple and certain. They are none the less valuable for that, and certainly none the less fundamental. The distinction of Macaulay's magnificent poem is that it enables the adult reader, or hearer, to recover in full some of the strong emotions of boyhood, an experience which is not a lapse from maturity but an endorsement of it.

For a number of reasons, a poet of our own day cannot write like that – in fact, during the 1930s this entire literary genre quite suddenly disappeared, never to return. Such a poet would almost certainly lack in the first place the required skill and application. Should he possess these, he would even so find himself using a dead style and forms. Clarity, heavy rhythms, strong rhymes and the rest are the vehicles of confidence, of a kind of innocence, of shared faiths and other long-extinct states of mind. The two great themes of popular verse were the nation and the Church, neither of which, to say the least, confers much sense of community any longer. Minor themes, like admiration of or desire for a simple rustic existence, have just been forgotten. The most obvious cause of it all is the disintegrative shock of the Great War.

I thought at first of grouping the poems by subject, but was defeated by a shortage both of categories and of poems that fitted squarely into one and only one. (I should perhaps explain here to readers under forty that the generous selection of war and battle pieces is due not so much to national belligerence as to the fact that their fellow-countrymen used to feel peculiarly united at such times. The feeling persisted for some years after it had become impossible to write patriotic verse.) So – the poems are arranged chronologically instead, according to the years of their authors' births. Although this is not a perfect plan, it has the advantage of offering a view not only of literary development but also of parts of our history. Read in this way, too, some poems shed an interesting, even ironical, light on those that precede or follow them.

ANONYMOUS

Hierusalem, My Happy Home

Hierusalem, my happy home,
  When shall I come to thee?
When shall my sorrows have an end
  Thy joys when shall I see?

O happy harbour of the saints,
  O sweet and pleasant soil
In thee no sorrow may be found
  No grief, no care, no toil.

No dampish mist is seen in thee,
  Nor cold nor darksome night;
There every soul shines as the sun,
  There God himself gives light.

There lust and lucre cannot dwell,
  There envy bears no sway;
There is no hunger, heat nor cold,
  But pleasure every way.

Hierusalem, Hierusalem,
  God grant I once may see
Thy endless joys, and of the same
  Partaker aye to be.

Thy walls are made of precious stones,
  Thy bulwarks diamonds square;
Thy gates are of right orient pearl,
  Exceeding rich and rare.

Thy turrets and thy pinnacles
  With carbuncles do shine;
Thy very streets are paved with gold,
  Surpassing clear and fine.

Thy houses are of ivory,
  Thy windows crystal clear,

Thy tiles are made of beaten gold,
 O God, that I were there.

Within thy gates doth nothing come
 That is not passing clean;
No spider's web, no dirt, no dust,
 No filth may there be seen.

Ah, my sweet home, Hierusalem,
 Would God I were in thee!
Would God my woes were at an end,
 Thy joys that I might see!

Thy gardens and thy gallant walks
 Continually are green;
There grows such sweet and pleasant flowers
 As nowhere else are seen.

Quite through the streets with silver sound
 The flood of life doth flow;
Upon whose banks on every side
 The wood of life doth grow.

There trees for evermore bear fruit
 And evermore do spring;
There evermore the angels sit
 And evermore do sing.

There David stands with harp in hand
 As master of the Quire;
Ten thousand times that man were blest
 That might this music hear.

Our Lady sings *Magnificat*
 With tune surpassing sweet;
And all the virgins bear their parts
 Sitting about her feet.

Te Deum doth Saint Ambrose sing,
 Saint Austin doth the like;
Old Simeon and Zachary
 Have not their songs to seek.

There Magdalen hath left her moan
    And cheerfully doth sing,
With blessed saints whose harmony
    In every street doth ring.

Hierusalem, my happy home,
    Would God I were in thee!
Would God my woes were at an end,
    Thy joys that I might see!

Edward, Edward

Why does your brand so drop with blood,
    Edward, Edward?
Why does your brand so drop with blood?
    And why so sad go ye, oh?
Oh, I have killed my hawk so good,
    Mother, mother:
Oh, I have killed my hawk so good:
    And I had no more but he, oh.

Your hawkës blood was never so red,
    Edward, Edward;
Your hawkës blood was never so red,
    My dear son I tell thee, oh.
Oh, I have killed my red-roan steed,
    Mother, mother:
Oh, I have killed my red-roan steed
    That erst was so fair and free, oh.

Your steed was old, and ye have got more,
    Edward, Edward;
Your steed was old, and ye have got more;
    Some other dole ye dree, oh.
Oh, I have killed my father dear,
    Mother, mother:
Oh, I have killed my father dear,
    Alas and woe is me, oh.

And whatten penance will ye dree for that,
    Edward, Edward?
And whatten penance will ye dree for that?
  My dear son, now tell me, oh.
I'll set my feet in yonder boat,
    Mother, mother:
I'll set my feet in yonder boat,
  And I'll fare over the sea, oh.

And what will ye do with your towers and your hall,
    Edward, Edward?
And what will ye do with your towers and your hall
  That were so fair to see, oh?
I'll let them stand till they down fall,
    Mother, mother:
I'll let them stand till they down fall,
  For here never more maun I be, oh.

And what will ye leave to your bairns and your wife,
    Edward, Edward?
And what will ye leave to your bairns and your wife
  When ye go over the sea, oh?
The worldës room, let them beg through life,
    Mother, mother:
The worldës room, let them beg through life,
  For them never more will I see, oh.

And what will ye leave to your own mother dear,
    Edward, Edward?
And what will ye leave to your own mother dear?
  My dear son, now tell me, oh.
The curse of hell from me shall ye bear,
    Mother, mother:
The curse of hell from me shall ye bear,
  Such counsels ye gave to me, oh.

Sir Patrick Spens

The king sits in Dumferlin town
  Drinking the blood-red wine:

Oh where will I get a good sailor
  To sail this ship of mine?

Up and spake an eldern knight
  Sat at the king's right knee:
Sir Patrick Spens is the best sailor
  That sails upon the sea.

The king has written a broad letter
  And signed it with his hand,
And sent it to Sir Patrick Spens
  Was walking on the strand.

To Noroway, to Noroway,
  To Noroway o'er the foam,
The king's daughter to Noroway,
  'Tis thou maun bring her home.

The first line that Sir Patrick read
  A loud laugh laughed he;
The next line that Sir Patrick read
  A tear blinded his eye.

Oh who is this has done this deed,
  This ill deed done to me,
To send me out this time of the year
  To sail upon the sea?

Make haste, make haste, my merry men all;
  Our good ship sails the morn.
Oh say not so, my master dear,
  For I fear a deadly storm.

Late, late yestreen I saw the new moon
  With the old moon in her arm,
And I fear, I fear, my master dear,
  That we will come to harm.

They hadna sailed a league, a league,
  A league but barely three,
When the air grew dark, and the wind blew loud,
  And growly grew the sea.

Oh our Scotch nobles were right loth
   To wet their cork-heeled shoon,
But long ere all the play were played
   Their hats they swam aboon.

Oh long, long may their ladies sit
   With their fans into their hand
Ere ever they see Sir Patrick Spens
   Come sailing to the land.

Oh long, long may the ladies stand
   With their gold combs in their hair
Waiting for their own dear lords,
   For they'll see them no more.

Half o'er, half o'er to Aberdour
   It's fifty fathom deep,
And there lies good Sir Patrick Spens
   With the Scotch lords at his feet.

Brave Lord Willoughby

The fifteenth day of July,
   With glistering spear and shield,
A famous fight in Flanders
   Was foughten in the field:
The most conspicuous officers
   Were English captains three,
But the bravest man in battle
   Was brave Lord Willoughby.

The next was Captain Norris,
   A valiant man was he:
The other, Captain Turner,
   From field would never flee.
With fifteen hundred fighting men,
   Alas! there were no more,
They fought with forty thousand then
   Upon the bloody shore.

'Stand to it, noble pikemen,
  And look you round about:
And shoot you right, you bow-men,
  And we will keep them out:
You musquet and caleever men,
  Do you prove true to me,
I'll be the bravest man in fight,'
  Says brave Lord Willoughby.

And then the bloody enemy
  They fiercely did assail,
And fought it out most furiously,
  Not doubting to prevail:
The wounded men on both sides fell
  Most piteous for to see,
But nothing could the courage quell
  Of brave Lord Willoughby.

For seven hours to all men's view
  This fight endurèd sore,
Until our men so feeble grew
  That they could fight no more;
And then upon dead horses
  Full savourly they eat,
And drank the puddle water:
  They could no better get.

When they had fed so freely,
  They kneelèd on the ground,
And praisèd God devoutly
  For the favour they had found;
And bearing up their colours,
  The fight they did renew,
And cutting towards the Spaniard,
  Five thousand more they slew.

The sharp steel-pointed arrows
  And bullets thick did fly;
Then did our valiant soldiers
  Charge on most furiously:
Which made the Spaniards waver,

They thought it best to flee:
They feared the stout behaviour
  Of brave Lord Willoughby.

Then quoth the Spanish general,
  'Come, let us march away,
I fear we shall be spoilèd all
  If that we longer stay:
For yonder comes Lord Willoughby
  With courage fierce and fell,
He will not give one inch of ground
  For all the devils in hell.'

And when the fearful enemy
  Was quickly put to flight,
Our men pursued courageously
  To rout his forces quite;
And at last they gave a shout
  Which echoed through the sky:
'God, and St. George for England!'
  The conquerors did cry.

This news was brought to England
  With all the speed might be,
And soon our gracious Queen was told
  Of this same victory.
'O! this is brave Lord Willoughby,
  My love that ever won:
Of all the lords of honour
  'Tis he great deeds hath done!'

To the soldiers that were maimèd,
  And wounded in the fray,
The queen allowed a pension
  Of fifteen pence a day,
And from all costs and charges
  She quit and set them free:
And this she did all for the sake
  Of brave Lord Willoughby.

Then courage, noble Englishmen,
  And never be dismayed!
If that we be but one to ten,
  We will not be afraid
To fight with foreign enemies,
  And set our country free.
And thus I end the bloody bout
  Of brave Lord Willoughby.

WILLIAM KETHE

The Old Hundredth

All people that on earth do dwell,
  Sing to the Lord with cheerful voice;
Him serve with mirth, his praise forth tell,
  Come ye before him, and rejoice.

The Lord, ye know, is God indeed;
  Without our aid he did us make;
We are his folk, he doth us feed,
  And for his sheep he doth us take.

O enter then his gates with praise;
  Approach with joy his courts unto;
Praise, laud, and bless his name always,
  For it is seemly so to do.

For why, the Lord our God is good:
  His mercy is for ever sure;
His truth at all times firmly stood,
  And shall from age to age endure.

To Father, Son, and Holy Ghost,
  The God whom heaven and earth adore,
From men and from the angel-host
  Be praise and glory evermore.

MICHAEL DRAYTON

Agincourt

Fair stood the wind for France,
When we our sails advance,
Nor now to prove our chance
    Longer will tarry;
But putting to the main,
At Caux, the mouth of Seine,
With all his martial train,
    Landed King Harry.

And taking many a fort,
Furnished in warlike sort,
Marched towards Agincourt
    In happy hour,
Skirmishing day by day
With those that stopped his way,
Where the French gen'ral lay
    With all his power:

Which, in his height of pride,
King Henry to deride,
His ransom to provide
    To the king sending;
Which he neglects the while
As from a nation vile,
Yet with an angry smile
    Their fall portending.

And turning to his men,
Quoth our brave Henry then,
'Though they to one be ten,
    Be not amazèd.
Yet have we well begun,
Battles so bravely won
Have ever to the sun
    By fame been raisèd.

And for myself, quoth he,
This my full rest shall be:

England ne'er mourn for me,
   Nor more esteem me;
Victor I will remain
Or on this earth lie slain;
Never shall she sustain
   Loss to redeem me.

Poitiers and Cressy tell,
When most their pride did swell,
Under our swords they fell;
   No less our skill is
Than when our grandsire great,
Claiming the regal seat,
By many a warlike feat
   Lopped the French lilies.'

The Duke of York so dread
The eager vaward led;
With the main Henry sped,
   Amongst his henchmen;
Excester had the rear,
A braver man not there:
O Lord, how hot they were
   On the false Frenchmen!

They now to fight are gone,
Armour on armour shone,
Drum now to drum did groan,
   To hear was wonder;
That with the cries they make
The very earth did shake,
Trumpet to trumpet spake,
   Thunder to thunder.

Well it thine age became,
O noble Erpingham,
Which did the signal aim
   To our hid forces!
When from a meadow by,
Like a storm suddenly,
The English archery
   Struck the French horses.

With Spanish yew so strong,
Arrows a cloth-yard long,
That like to serpents stung,
    Piercing the weather;
None from his fellow starts,
But playing manly parts,
And like true English hearts
    Stuck close together.

When down their bows they threw,
And forth their bilbos drew,
And on the French they flew,
    Not one was tardy;
Arms were from shoulders sent,
Scalps to the teeth were rent,
Down the French peasants went;
    Our men were hardy.

This while our noble king,
His broadsword brandishing,
Down the French host did ding
    As to o'erwhelm it,
And many a deep wound lent,
His arms with blood besprent,
And many a cruel dent
    Bruisèd his helmet.

Glo'ster, that duke so good,
Next of the royal blood,
For famous England stood,
    With his brave brother;
Clarence, in steel so bright,
Though but a maiden knight,
Yet in that furious fight
    Scarce such another!

Warwick in blood did wade,
Oxford the foe invade,
And cruel slaughter made,
    Still as they ran up;

Suffolk his axe did ply,
Beaumont and Willoughby
Bare them right doughtily,
    Ferrers and Fanhope.

Upon Saint Crispin's Day
Fought was this noble fray,
Which fame did not delay,
    To England to carry.
O, when shall Englishmen
With such acts fill a pen,
Or England breed again
    Such a King Harry?

WILLIAM SHAKESPEARE

All the World's a Stage

All the world's a stage,
And all the men and women merely players:
They have their exits and their entrances;
And one man in his time plays many parts,
His acts being seven ages. At first the infant,
Mewling and puking in the nurse's arms.
And then the whining schoolboy, with his satchel,
And shining morning face, creeping like snail
Unwillingly to school. And then the lover,
Sighing like furnace, with a woeful ballad
Made to his mistress' eyebrow. Then a soldier,
Full of strange oaths, and bearded like the pard,
Jealous in honour, sudden and quick in quarrel,
Seeking the bubble reputation
Even in the cannon's mouth. And then the justice,
In fair round belly with good capon lined,
With eyes severe and beard of formal cut,
Full of wise saws and modern instances;
And so he plays his part. The sixth age shifts
Into the lean and slippered pantaloon,
With spectacles on nose, and pouch on side;
His youthful hose, well saved, a world too wide

For his shrunk shank; and his big manly voice,
Turning again toward childish treble, pipes
And whistles in his sound. Last scene of all,
That ends this strange eventful history,
Is second childishness and mere oblivion,
Sans teeth, sans eyes, sans taste, sans everything.

John of Gaunt Speaks

This royal throne of kings, this sceptered isle,
This earth of majesty, this seat of Mars,
This other Eden, demi-paradise,
This fortress, built by nature for herself,
Against infection and the hand of war;
This happy breed of men, this little world;
This precious stone set in the silver sea,
Which serves it in the office of a wall
Or as a moat defensive to a house,
Against the envy of less happier lands;
This blessed plot, this earth, this realm, this England,
This nurse, this teeming womb of royal kings,
Feared by their breed and famous by their birth,
Renowned for their deeds as far from home,
For Christian service and true chivalry,
As is the sepulchre in stubborn Jewry,
Of the world's ransom, blessed Mary's son;
This land of such dear souls, this dear dear land,
Dear for her reputation through the world,
Is now leased out, I die pronouncing it,
Like to a tenement or pelting farm:
England, bound in with the triumphant sea,
Whose rocky shore beats back the envious siege,
Of watery Neptune, is now bound in with shame,
With inky blots, and rotten parchment bonds;
That England, that was wont to conquer others,
Hath made a shameful conquest of itself:
Ah, would the scandal vanish with my life,
How happy then were my ensuing death!

Henry V before Agincourt

This day is called the feast of Crispian:
He that outlives this day and comes safe home,
Will stand a tip-toe when this day is named,
And rouse him at the name of Crispian.
He that shall see this day, and live old age,
Will yearly on the vigil feast his neighbours,
And say, 'to-morrow is Saint Crispian:'
Then will he strip his sleeve and show his scars:
Old men forget; yet all shall be forgot,
But he'll remember, with advantages,
What feats he did that day: then shall our names,
Familiar in his mouth as household words,
Harry the king, Bedford and Exeter,
Warwick and Talbot, Salisbury and Gloucester,
Be in their flowing cups freshly remembered:
This story shall the good man teach his son;
And Crispin Crispian shall ne'er go by,
From this day to the ending of the world,
But we in it shall be remembered:
We few, we happy few, we band of brothers;
For he to-day that sheds his blood with me
Shall be my brother; be he ne'er so vile
This day shall gentle his condition:
And gentlemen in England, now a-bed,
Shall think themselves accursed they were not here;
And hold their manhoods cheap, whiles any speaks
That fought with us upon Saint Crispin's day.

Mark Antony Addresses the Mob

Friends, Romans, countrymen, lend me your ears;
I come to bury Cæsar, not to praise him.
The evil that men do lives after them;
The good is oft interred with their bones;
So let it be with Cæsar. The noble Brutus
Hath told you Cæsar was ambitious:
If it were so, it was a grievous fault;

And grievously hath Cæsar answered it.
Here, under leave of Brutus, and the rest,
For Brutus is an honourable man;
So are they all, all honourable men;
Come I to speak in Cæsar's funeral.
He was my friend, faithful and just to me:
But Brutus says, he was ambitious;
And Brutus is an honourable man.
He hath brought many captives home to Rome,
Whose ransoms did the general coffers fill:
Did this in Cæsar seem ambitious?
When that the poor have cried, Cæsar hath wept:
Ambition should be made of sterner stuff:
Yet Brutus says, he was ambitious;
And Brutus is an honourable man.
You all did see that on the Lupercal
I thrice presented him a kingly crown,
Which he did thrice refuse. Was this ambition?
Yet Brutus says, he was ambitious;
And, sure, he is an honourable man.
I speak not to disprove what Brutus spoke,
But here I am to speak what I do know.
You all did love him once, not without cause;
What cause withholds you then to mourn for him?
O judgment, thou art fled to brutish beasts,
And men have lost their reason! Bear with me;
My heart is in the coffin there with Cæsar,
And I must pause till it come back to me.

*

If you have tears, prepare to shed them now.
You all do know this mantle: I remember
The first time ever Cæsar put it on;
'Twas on a summer's evening, in his tent,
That day he overcame the Nervii:
Look, in this place ran Cassius' dagger through:
See what a rent the envious Casca made:
Through this, the well-beloved Brutus stabbed;
And as he plucked his cursed steel away,
Mark how the blood of Cæsar followed it,
As rushing out of doors, to be resolved

If Brutus so unkindly knocked, or no;
For Brutus, as you know, was Cæsar's angel:
Judge, O you gods, how dearly Cæsar loved him!
This was the most unkindest cut of all:
For when the noble Cæsar saw him stab,
Ingratitude, more strong than traitors' arms,
Quite vanquished him: then burst his mighty heart;
And, in his mantle muffling up his face,
Even at the base of Pompey's statuë,
Which all the while ran blood, great Cæsar fell.
O, what a fall was there, my countrymen!
Then I, and you, and all of us fell down,
Whilst bloody treason flourished over us.
O, now you weep, and I perceive you feel
The dint of pity: these are gracious drops.
Kind souls, what weep you when you but behold
Our Cæsar's vesture wounded? Look you here,
Here is himself, marred, as you see, with traitors.

THOMAS CAMPION

Jack and Joan

Jack and Joan they think no ill,
But loving live, and merry still;
Do their week-days' work, and pray
Devoutly on the holy day;
Skip and trip it on the green,
And help to choose the Summer Queen;
Lash out at a country feast
Their silver penny with the best.

Well can they judge of nappy ale,
And tell at large a winter tale;
Climb up to the apple loft,
And turn the crabs till they be soft.
Tib is all the father's joy,
And little Tom the mother's boy.
All their pleasure is content,
And care to pay their yearly rent.

Joan can call by name her cows,
And deck her windows with green boughs;
She can wreaths and tutties make,
And trim with plums a bridal cake.
Jack knows what brings gain or loss,
And his long flail can stoutly toss;
Make the hedge which others break,
And ever thinks what he doth speak.

Now you courtly dames and knights,
That study only strange delights,
Though you scorn the home-spun gray
And revel in your rich array;
Though your tongues dissemble deep
And can your heads from danger keep:
Yet for all your pomp and train,
Securer lives the silly swain.

THOMAS NASHE

In Plague Time

Adieu, farewell earth's bliss,
This world uncertain is;
Fond are life's lustful joys,
Death proves them all but toys,
None from his darts can fly.
I am sick, I must die.
  Lord, have mercy on us!

Rich men, trust not in wealth,
Gold cannot buy you health;
Physic himself must fade,
All things to end are made.
The plague full swift goes by.
I am sick, I must die.
  Lord, have mercy on us!

Beauty is but a flower
Which wrinkles will devour;

36

Brightness falls from the air,
Queens have died young and fair,
Dust hath closed Helen's eye.
I am sick, I must die.
  Lord, have mercy on us!

Strength stoops unto the grave,
Worms feed on Hector brave,
Swords may not fight with fate,
Earth still holds ope her gate.
Come! come! the bells do cry.
I am sick, I must die.
  Lord, have mercy on us!

Wit with his wantonness
Tasteth death's bitterness;
Hell's executioner
Hath no ears for to hear
What vain art can reply.
I am sick, I must die.
  Lord, have mercy on us!

Haste, therefore, each degree,
To welcome destiny.
Heaven is our heritage,
Earth but a player's stage;
Mount we unto the sky.
I am sick, I must die.
  Lord, have mercy on us!

SIR HENRY WOTTON

The Character of a Happy Life

How happy is he born and taught
That serveth not another's will;
Whose armour is his honest thought,
And simple truth his utmost skill!

Whose passions not his masters are;
Whose soul is still prepared for death,
Untied unto the world by care
Of public fame or private breath;

Who envies none that chance doth raise,
Nor vice; who never understood
How deepest wounds are given by praise;
Nor rules of state, but rules of good;

Who hath his life from rumours freed;
Whose conscience is his strong retreat;
Whose state can neither flatterers feed,
Nor ruin make oppressors great;

Who God doth late and early pray
More of His grace than gifts to lend;
And entertains the harmless day
With a religious book or friend;

—This man is freed from servile bands
Of hope to rise or fear to fall:
Lord of himself, though not of lands,
And having nothing, yet hath all.

FRANCIS BEAUMONT

In Westminster Abbey

Mortality, behold and fear!
What a change of flesh is here!
Think how many royal bones
Sleep beneath this heap of stones!
Here they lie had realms and lands,
Who now want strength to stir their hands
Here from their pulpits sealed with dust
They preach, 'In greatness is no trust.'
Here is an acre sown indeed
With the richest, royall'st seed
That the earth did e'er suck in,

Since the first man died for sin.
Here the bones of birth have cried,
'Though gods they were, as men they died.'
Here are sands, ignoble things,
Dropt from the ruined sides of kings.
Here's a world of pomp and state,
Buried in dust, once dead by fate.

JAMES SHIRLEY

Death the Leveller

The glories of our blood and state
  Are shadows, not substantial things;
There is no armour against Fate;
  Death lays his icy hand on kings:
        Sceptre and Crown
        Must tumble down,
And in the dust be equal made
With the poor crooked scythe and spade.

Some men with swords may reap the field,
  And plant fresh laurels where they kill:
But their strong nerves at last must yield;
  They tame but one another still:
        Early or late
        They stoop to fate,
And must give up their murmuring breath
When they, pale captives, creep to death.

The garlands wither on your brow;
  Then boast no more your mighty deeds!
Upon Death's purple altar now
  See where the victor-victim bleeds.
        Your heads must come
        To the cold tomb:
Only the actions of the just
Smell sweet and blossom in their dust.

JOHN MILTON

On His Blindness

When I consider how my light is spent,
  Ere half my days, in this dark world and wide,
  And that one talent which is death to hide,
  Lodged with me useless, though my soul more bent
To serve therewith my maker, and present
  My true account, lest he returning chide,
  Doth God exact day-labour, light denied,
  I fondly ask; but Patience to prevent
That murmur, soon replies, God doth not need
  Either man's work or his own gifts, who best
  Bear his mild yoke, they serve him best, his state
Is kingly. Thousands at his bidding speed
  And post o'er land and ocean without rest:
  They also serve who only stand and wait.

JOHN BUNYAN

To Be a Pilgrim

He who would valiant be
    'Gainst all disaster,
Let him in constancy
    Follow the Master.
There's no discouragement
Shall make him once relent
His first avowed intent
    To be a pilgrim.

Who so beset him round
    With dismal stories,
Do but themselves confound—
    His strength the more is.
No foes shall stay his might,
Though he with giants fight:
He will make good his right
    To be a pilgrim.

Since, Lord, thou dost defend
　　Us with thy Spirit,
We know we at the end
　　Shall life inherit.
Then fancies flee away!
I'll fear not what men say,
I'll labour night and day
　　To be a pilgrim.

JOHN DRYDEN

Alexander's Feast

'Twas at the royal feast for Persia won
　　By Philip's warlike son:
　　　Aloft in awful state
　　　The godlike hero sate
　　　On his imperial throne;
His valiant peers were placed around,
Their brows with roses and with myrtles bound
　(So should desert in arms be crowned);
The lovely Thais by his side
Sate like a blooming Eastern bride
In flower of youth and beauty's pride.
　　Happy, happy, happy pair!
　　　None but the brave,
　　　None but the brave,
　None but the brave deserves the fair!

　　Timotheus, placed on high
　　　Amid the tuneful quire,
With flying fingers touched the lyre:
　　The trembling notes ascend the sky
　　And heavenly joys inspire.
The song began from Jove
Who left his blissful seats above,
Such is the power of mighty love!
A dragon's fiery form belied the god;
Sublime on radiant spires he rode

41

When he to fair Olympia pressed,
And while he sought her snowy breast,
Then round her slender waist he curled,
And stamped an image of himself, a sovereign of the world.
The listening crowd admire the lofty sound;
A present deity! they shout around:
A present deity! the vaulted roofs rebound:
   With ravished ears
   The monarch hears,
   Assumes the god;
   Affects to nod
And seems to shake the spheres.

The praise of Bacchus then the sweet musician sung,
 Of Bacchus ever fair and ever young:
  The jolly god in triumph comes;
  Sound the trumpets, beat the drums!
   Flushed with a purple grace
   He shows his honest face:
Now give the hautboys breath; he comes, he comes!
  Bacchus, ever fair and young,
   Drinking joys did first ordain;
  Bacchus' blessings are a treasure,
  Drinking is the soldier's pleasure:
   Rich the treasure,
   Sweet the pleasure,
  Sweet is pleasure after pain.

 Soothed with the sound the king grew vain;
  Fought all his battles o'er again,
And thrice he routed all his foes, and thrice he slew the slain!
  The master saw the madness rise,
  His glowing cheeks, his ardent eyes;
  And while he heaven and earth defied
  Changed his hand, and checked his pride.
   He chose a mournful Muse
   Soft pity to infuse:
  He sung Darius great and good,
   By too severe a fate
  Fallen, fallen, fallen, fallen,
   Fallen from his high estate,

And weltering in his blood;
Deserted at his utmost need
By those his former bounty fed,
On the bare earth exposed he lies
With not a friend to close his eyes.
With downcast looks the joyless victor sate,
 Revolving in his altered soul
  The various turns of Chance below;
 And now and then a sigh he stole,
 And tears began to flow.

The mighty master smiled to see
That love was in the next degree;
'Twas but a kindred-sound to move,
For pity melts the mind to love.
 Softly sweet, in Lydian measures
 Soon he soothed his soul to pleasures.
War, he sang, is toil and trouble,
Honour but an empty bubble;
 Never ending, still beginning,
Fighting still, and still destroying;
 If the world be worth thy winning,
Think, O think, it worth enjoying:
 Lovely Thais sits beside thee,
 Take the good the gods provide thee.
The many rend the skies with loud applause;
So love was crowned, but Music won the cause.
 The prince, unable to conceal his pain,
  Gazed on the fair
  Who caused his care,
 And sighed and looked, sighed and looked,
 Sighed and looked, and sighed again:
At length, with love and wine at once oppressed,
The vanquished victor sunk upon her breast.

Now strike the golden lyre again:
A louder yet, and yet a louder strain!
Break his bands of sleep asunder
And rouse him like a rattling peal of thunder.
 Hark, hark! the horrid sound
 Has raised up his head:

43

As awaked from the dead,
And amazed he stares around.
Revenge, revenge, Timotheus cries,
    See the Furies arise!
    See the snakes that they rear,
    How they hiss in their hair,
And the sparkles that flash from their eyes!
    Behold a ghastly band,
    Each a torch in his hand!
Those are Grecian ghosts, that in battle were slain
            And unburied remain
            Inglorious on the plain:
            Give the vengeance due
            To the valiant crew!
Behold how they toss their torches on high,
    How they point to the Persian abodes
And glittering temples of their hostile gods.
The princes applaud with a furious joy:
And the King seized a flambeau with zeal to destroy;
            Thais led the way
            To light him to his prey,
And like another Helen fired another Troy!

            Thus long ago,
    Ere heaving bellows learned to blow,
        While organs yet were mute,
        Timotheus, to his breathing flute
            And sounding lyre,
Could swell the soul to rage or kindle soft desire.
    At last divine Cecilia came,
    Inventress of the vocal frame;
The sweet enthusiast from her sacred store
    Enlarged the former narrow bounds,
    And added length to solemn sounds,
With Nature's mother-wit and arts unknown before.
    Let old Timotheus yield the prize,
        Or both divide the crown:
    He raised a mortal to the skies;
        She drew an angel down.

Happy the Man

Happy the man, and happy he alone,
   He who can call today his own:
   He who, secure within, can say,
Tomorrow do thy worst, for I have lived today.
   Be fair or foul or rain or shine
The joys I have possessed, in spite of fate, are mine.
Not Heaven itself upon the past has power,
But what has been, has been, and I have had my hour.

Veni, Creator Spiritus

Creator Spirit, by whose aid
The world's foundations first were laid,
Come, visit every pious mind;
Come, pour thy joys on human kind;
From sin and sorrow set us free,
And make thy temples worthy thee.

O source of uncreated light,
The Father's promised Paraclete,
Thrice holy fount, thrice holy fire,
Our hearts with heavenly love inspire;
Come, and thy sacred unction bring
To sanctify us while we sing.

Plenteous of grace, descend from high
Rich in thy sevenfold energy;
Make us eternal truths receive,
And practise all that we believe;
Give us thyself, that we may see
The Father and the Son by thee.

Immortal honour, endless fame,
Attend the almighty Father's name;
The saviour Son be glorified,
Who for lost man's redemption died;
And equal adoration be,
Eternal Paraclete, to thee.

ANONYMOUS

The Boyne Water

July the First, of a morning clear, one thousand six hundred
 and ninety,
King William did his men prepare, of thousands he had thirty;
To fight King James and all his foes, encamped near the Boyne
 Water,
He little fear'd though two to one, their multitudes to scatter.

King William call'd his officers, saying: 'Gentlemen, mind
 your station,
And let your valour here be shown before this Irish nation;
My brazen walls let no man break, and your subtle foes you'll
 scatter,
Be sure you show them good English play as you go over the
 water.'

Both foot and horse they marched on, intending them to
 batter,
But the brave Duke Schomberg he was shot as he cross'd over
 the water.
When that King William did observe the brave Duke
 Schomberg falling,
He rein'd his horse with a heavy heart, on the Enniskilleners
 calling:

'What will you do for me, brave boys – see yonder men
 retreating?
Our enemies encourag'd are and English drums are beating;'
He says, 'My boys, feel no dismay at the losing of one
 commander,
For God shall be our king this day, and I'll be general under.'

Within four yards of our fore-front, before a shot was fired,
A sudden snuff they got that day, which little they desired;
For horse and man fell to the ground, and some hung in their
 saddle;
Others turn'd up their forked ends, which we call 'coup de
 ladle.'

Prince Eugene's regiment was the next, on our right hand
    advanced,
Into a field of standing wheat, where Irish horses pranced—
But the brandy ran so in their heads, their senses all did scatter,
They little thought to leave their bones that day at the Boyne
    Water.

Both men and horse lay on the ground, and many there lay
    bleeding;
I saw no sickles there that day – but, sure, there was sharp
    shearing.

Now, praise God, all true Protestants, and heaven's and earth's
    Creator,
For the deliverance that He sent our enemies to scatter.
The Church's foes will pine away, like churlish-hearted Nabal,
For our deliverer came this day like the great Zorobabel.

So praise God, all true Protestants, and I will say no further,
But had the Papists gain'd the day there would have been
    open murder.
Although King James and many more were ne'er that way
    inclined,
It was not in their power to stop what the rabble they
    designed.

JOSEPH ADDISON

The Spacious Firmament on High

The spacious firmament on high,
With all the blue ethereal sky,
And spangled heavens, a shining frame,
Their great Original proclaim.
The unwearied sun from day to day
Does his Creator's power display,
And publishes to every land
The works of an almighty hand.

Soon as the evening shades prevail
The moon takes up the wondrous tale,

And nightly to the listening earth
Repeats the story of her birth;
Whilst all the stars that round her burn
And all the planets in their turn,
Confirm the tidings, as they roll,
And spread the truth from pole to pole.

What though in solemn silence all
Move round the dark terrestrial ball;
What though nor real voice nor sound
Amid their radiant orbs be found;
In reason's ear they all rejoice,
And utter forth a glorious voice;
For ever singing as they shine,
'The hand that made us is divine.'

ISAAC WATTS

O God, Our Help in Ages Past

O God, our help in ages past,
   Our hope for years to come,
Our shelter from the stormy blast,
   And our eternal home;

Under the shadow of thy throne
   Thy saints have dwelt secure;
Sufficient is thine arm alone,
   And our defence is sure.

Before the hills in order stood,
   Or earth received her frame,
From everlasting thou art God,
   To endless years the same.

A thousand ages in thy sight
   Are like an evening gone,
Short as the watch that ends the night
   Before the rising sun.

Time, like an ever-rolling stream,
    Bears all its sons away;
They fly forgotten, as a dream
    Dies at the opening day.

O God, our help in ages past,
    Our hope for years to come,
Be thou our guard while troubles last,
    And our eternal home.

When I Survey the Wondrous Cross

When I survey the wondrous cross,
    On which the Prince of Glory died,
My richest gain I count but loss,
    And pour contempt on all my pride.

Forbid it, Lord, that I should boast
    Save in the death of Christ my God;
All the vain things that charm me most,
    I sacrifice them to his blood.

See from his head, his hands, his feet,
    Sorrow and love flow mingled down;
Did e'er such love and sorrow meet,
    Or thorns compose so rich a crown?

His dying crimson, like a robe,
    Spreads o'er his body on the tree;
Then am I dead to all the globe,
    And all the globe is dead to me.

Were the whole realm of nature mine,
    That were a present far too small;
Love so amazing, so divine,
    Demands my soul, my life, my all.

JAMES THOMSON

Rule, Britannia

When Britain first, at heaven's command,
  Arose from out the azure main;
This was the charter of the land,
  And guardian Angels sung this strain:
    'Rule, Britannia, rule the waves;
    Britons never will be slaves.'

The nations, not so blest as thee,
  Must, in their turns, to tyrants fall:
While thou shalt flourish great and free,
  The dread and envy of them all.
    'Rule, etc.

Still more majestic shalt thou rise,
  More dreadful, from each foreign stroke:
As the loud blast that tears the skies,
  Serves but to root thy native oak.
    'Rule, etc.

Thee haughty tyrants ne'er shall tame:
  All their attemps to bend thee down,
Will but arouse thy generous flame;
  But work their woe, and thy renown.
    'Rule, etc.

To thee belongs the rural reign;
  Thy cities shall with commerce shine:
All thine shall be the subject main,
  And every shore it circles thine.
    'Rule. etc.

The Muses, still with freedom found,
  Shall to thy happy coast repair:
Blest isle! with matchless beauty crowned,
  And manly hearts to guard the fair.
    'Rule, Britannia, rule the waves:
    Britons never will be slaves.'

CHARLES WESLEY

Jesu, Lover of My Soul

Jesu, lover of my soul,
  Let me to thy bosom fly,
While the nearer waters roll,
  While the tempest still is high:
Hide me, O my Saviour, hide,
  Till the storm of life is past;
Safe into the haven guide,
  O receive my soul at last.

Other refuge have I none;
  Hangs my helpless soul on thee;
Leave, ah! leave me not alone,
  Still support and comfort me.
All my trust on thee is stayed,
  All my help from thee I bring;
Cover my defenceless head
  With the shadow of thy wing.

Plenteous grace with thee is found,
  Grace to cover all my sin;
Let the healing streams abound;
  Make and keep me pure within.
Thou of life the fountain art;
  Freely let me take of thee;
Spring thou up within my heart,
  Rise to all eternity.

SAMUEL JOHNSON

Prologue to 'A Word to the Wise'

This night presents a play which public rage,
Or right, or wrong, once hooted from the stage.
From zeal or malice, now no more we dread,
For English vengeance wars not with the dead.

A generous foe regards with pitying eye
The man whom fate has laid where all must lie.
To wit reviving from its author's dust,
Be kind, ye judges, or at least be just,
For no renew'd hostilities invade
The oblivious grave's inviolable shade.
Let one great payment every claim appease,
And him, who cannot hurt, allow to please;
To please by scenes unconscious of offence,
By harmless merriment or useful sense.
Where aught of bright, or fair, the piece displays,
Approve it only – 'tis too late to praise.
If want of skill, or want of care appear,
Forbear to hiss – the poet cannot hear.
By all, like him, must praise and blame be found,
At best a fleeting gleam, or empty sound.
Yet then shall calm reflection bless the night
When liberal pity dignify'd delight;
When pleasure fired her torch at Virtue's flame,
And Mirth was Bounty with an humbler name.

THOMAS GRAY

Elegy
Written in a Country Churchyard

The curfew tolls the knell of parting day,
The lowing herd wind slowly o'er the lea,
The ploughman homeward plods his weary way,
And leaves the world to darkness and to me.

Now fades the glimmering landscape on the sight,
And all the air a solemn stillness holds,
Save where the beetle wheels his droning flight,
And drowsy tinklings lull the distant folds;

Save that from yonder ivy-mantled tower
The moping owl does to the moon complain
Of such as, wandering near her secret bower,
Molest her ancient solitary reign.

Beneath those rugged elms, that yew-tree's shade,
Where heaves the turf in many a mouldering heap,
Each in his narrow cell for ever laid,
The rude forefathers of the hamlet sleep.

The breezy call of incense-breathing morn,
The swallow twittering from the straw-built shed,
The cock's shrill clarion or the echoing horn,
No more shall rouse them from their lowly bed.

For them no more the blazing hearth shall burn,
Or busy housewife ply her evening care:
No children run to lisp their sire's return,
Or climb his knees the envied kiss to share.

Oft did the harvest to their sickle yield,
Their furrow oft the stubborn glebe has broke;
How jocund did they drive their team afield!
How bowed the woods beneath their sturdy stroke!

Let not Ambition mock their useful toil,
Their homely joys and destiny obscure;
Nor Grandeur hear, with a disdainful smile,
The short and simple annals of the poor.

The boast of heraldry, the pomp of power,
And all that beauty, all that wealth e'er gave,
Awaits alike the inevitable hour.
The paths of glory lead but to the grave.

Nor you, ye Proud, impute to these the fault,
If Memory o'er their tomb no trophies raise,
Where through the long-drawn aisle and fretted vault
The pealing anthem swells the note of praise.

Can storied urn or animated bust
Back to its mansion call the fleeting breath?
Can Honour's voice provoke the silent dust,
Or Flattery soothe the dull cold ear of Death?

Perhaps in this neglected spot is laid
Some heart once pregnant with celestial fire;

Hands that the rod of empire might have swayed,
Or waked to ecstasy the living lyre.

But Knowledge to their eyes her ample page
Rich with the spoils of time did ne'er unroll;
Chill Penury repressed their noble rage,
And froze the genial current of the soul.

Full many a gem of purest ray serene
The dark unfathomed caves of ocean bear:
Full many a flower is born to blush unseen,
And waste its sweetness on the desert air.

Some village-Hampden that with dauntless breast
The little tyrant of his fields withstood;
Some mute inglorious Milton here may rest,
Some Cromwell guiltless of his country's blood.

The applause of listening senates to command,
The threats of pain and ruin to despise,
To scatter plenty o'er a smiling land,
And read their history in a nation's eyes,

Their lot forbade: nor circumscribed alone
Their growing virtues, but their crimes confined;
Forbade to wade through slaughter to a throne,
And shut the gates of mercy on mankind,

The struggling pangs of conscious truth to hide,
To quench the blushes of ingenuous shame,
Or heap the shrine of Luxury and Pride
With incense kindled at the Muse's flame.

Far from the madding crowd's ignoble strife
Their sober wishes never learned to stray;
Along the cool sequestered vale of life
They kept the noiseless tenor of their way.

Yet even these bones from insult to protect
Some frail memorial still erected nigh,
With uncouth rhymes and shapeless sculpture decked,
Implores the passing tribute of a sigh.

Their name, their years, spelt by the unlettered muse,
The place of fame and elegy supply:
And many a holy text around she strews,
That teach the rustic moralist to die.

For who to dumb Forgetfulness a prey,
This pleasing anxious being e'er resigned,
Left the warm precincts of the cheerful day,
Nor cast one longing lingering look behind?

On some fond breast the parting soul relies,
Some pious drops the closing eye requires;
Even from the tomb the voice of Nature cries,
Even in our ashes live their wonted fires.

For thee who, mindful of the unhonoured dead,
Dost in these lines their artless tale relate;
If chance, by lonely Contemplation led,
Some kindred spirit shall inquire thy fate,

Haply some hoary-headed swain may say,
'Oft have we seen him at the peep of dawn
Brushing with hasty steps the dews away
To meet the sun upon the upland lawn.

'There at the foot of yonder nodding beech
That wreathes its old fantastic roots so high,
His listless length at noontide would he stretch,
And pore upon the brook that babbles by.

'Hard by yon wood, now smiling as in scorn,
Muttering his wayward fancies he would rove,
Now drooping, woeful wan, like one forlorn,
Or crazed with care, or crossed in hopeless love.

'One morn I missed him on the customed hill,
Along the heath and near his favourite tree;
Another came; nor yet beside the rill,
Nor up the lawn, nor at the wood was he;

'The next with dirges due in sad array
Slow through the church-way path we saw him borne.
Approach and read (for thou canst read) the lay,
Graved on the stone beneath yon aged thorn.'

[THE EPITAPH]
Here rests his head upon the lap of earth
A youth to Fortune and to Fame unknown.
Fair Science frowned not on his humble birth,
And Melancholy marked him for her own.

Large was his bounty and his soul sincere,
Heaven did a recompense as largely send:
He gave to Misery all he had, a tear,
He gained from Heaven ('twas all he wished) a friend.

No farther seek his merits to disclose,
Or draw his frailties from their dread abode,
(There they alike in trembling hope repose)
The bosom of his Father and his God.

T. O. MORDAUNT

Sound, Sound the Clarion

Sound, sound the clarion, fill the fife!
  Throughout the sensual world proclaim,
One crowded hour of glorious life
  Is worth an age without a name.

WILLIAM COWPER

The Royal George

Toll for the Brave!
The brave that are no more!
All sunk beneath the wave
Fast by their native shore!

Eight hundred of the brave,
Whose courage well was tried,
Had made the vessel heel
And laid her on her side.

A land-breeze shook the shrouds
And she was overset;
Down went the Royal George
With all her crew complete.

Toll for the brave!
Brave Kempenfelt is gone;
His last sea-fight is fought,
His work of glory done.

It was not in the battle;
No tempest gave the shock;
She sprang no fatal leak,
She ran upon no rock.

His sword was in its sheath,
His fingers held the pen,
When Kempenfelt went down
With twice four hundred men.

Weigh the vessel up
Once dreaded by our foes!
And mingle with our cup
The tear that England owes.

Her timbers yet are sound,
And she may float again
Full charged with England's thunder,
And plough the distant main:

But Kempenfelt is gone,
His victories are o'er;
And he and his eight hundred
Shall plough the wave no more.

Boadicea

When the British warrior queen,
  Bleeding from the Roman rods,
Sought with an indignant mien
  Counsel of her country's gods,

Sage beneath the spreading oak
  Sat the Druid, hoary chief,
Every burning word he spoke
  Full of rage, and full of grief:

'Princess! if our aged eyes
  Weep upon thy matchless wrongs,
'Tis because resentment ties
  All the terrors of our tongues.

'Rome shall perish, – write that word
  In the blood that she has spilt;
Perish hopeless and abhorred,
  Deep in ruin as in guilt.

'Rome, for empire far renowned,
  Tramples on a thousand states;
Soon her pride shall kiss the ground, –
  Hark! the Gaul is at her gates!

'Other Romans shall arise
  Heedless of a soldier's name;
Sounds, not arms, shall win the prize,
  Harmony the path to fame.

'Then the progeny that springs
  From the forests of our land,
Armed with thunder, clad with wings,
  Shall a wider world command.

'Regions Cæsar never knew
  Thy posterity shall sway;
Where his eagles never flew,
  None invincible as they.'

Such the bard's prophetic words,
  Pregnant with celestial fire,
Bending as he swept the chords
  Of his sweet but awful lyre.

She with all a monarch's pride
  Felt them in her bosom glow,
Rushed to battle, fought, and died,
  Dying, hurled them at the foe:

'Ruffians, pitiless as proud,
  Heaven awards the vengeance due,
Empire is on us bestowed,
  Shame and ruin wait for you.'

A. M. TOPLADY

Rock of Ages

Rock of ages, cleft for me,
Let me hide myself in thee;
Let the water and the blood,
From thy riven side which flowed,
Be of sin the double cure:
Cleanse me from its guilt and power.

Not the labours of my hands
Can fulfil thy law's demands;
Could my zeal no respite know,
Could my tears for ever flow,
All for sin could not atone:
Thou must save, and thou alone.

Nothing in my hand I bring;
Simply to thy cross I cling;
Naked, come to thee for dress;
Helpless, look to thee for grace;
Foul, I to the fountain fly;
Wash me, Saviour, or I die.

While I draw this fleeting breath,
When mine eyes are closed in death,
When I soar through tracts unknown,
See thee on thy judgment throne;
Rock of ages, cleft for me,
Let me hide myself in thee.

PRINCE HOARE

The Arethusa

Come, all ye jolly sailors bold,
Whose hearts are cast in honour's mould,
While English glory I unfold,
     Huzza for the Arethusa!
She is a frigate tight and brave,
As ever stemmed the dashing wave;
     Her men are staunch
     To their fav'rite launch,
And when the foe shall meet our fire,
Sooner than strike, we'll all expire
     On board of the Arethusa.

'Twas with the spring fleet she went out
The English Channel to cruise about,
When four French sail, in show so stout
     Bore down on the Arethusa.
The famed Belle Poule straight ahead did lie,
The Arethusa seemed to fly,
     Not a sheet, or a tack,
     Or a brace, did she slack;
Though the Frenchman laughed and thought it stuff,
But they knew not the handful of men, how tough,
     On board of the Arethusa.

On deck five hundred men did dance,
The stoutest they could find in France;
We with two hundred did advance
     On board of the Arethusa.

Our captain hailed the Frenchman, 'Ho!'
The Frenchman then cried out 'Hallo!'
      'Bear down, d'ye see,
      To our Admiral's lee!'
'No, no,' says the Frenchman, 'that can't be!'
'Then I must lug you along with me,'
      Says the saucy Arethusa.

The fight was off the Frenchman's land,
We forced them back upon their strand,
For we fought till not a stick could stand
      Of the gallant Arethusa.
And now we've driven the foe ashore
Never to fight with Britons more,
      Let each fill his glass
      To his fav'rite lass;
A health to our captain and officers true,
And all that belong to the jovial crew
      On board of the Arethusa.

WILLIAM BLAKE

The Tiger

Tiger! Tiger! burning bright
In the forests of the night,
What immortal hand or eye
Could frame thy fearful symmetry?

In what distant deeps or skies
Burned the fire of thine eyes?
On what wings dare he aspire?
What the hand dare seize the fire?

And what shoulder, and what art,
Could twist the sinews of thy heart?
And when thy heart began to beat,
What dread hand? And what dread feet?

What the hammer? What the chain?
In what furnace was thy brain?

What the anvil? What dread grasp
Dare its deadly terrors clasp?

When the stars threw down their spears,
And watered heaven with their tears,
Did he smile his work to see?
Did he who made the Lamb make thee?

Tiger! Tiger! burning bright
In the forests of the night,
What immortal hand or eye
Dare frame thy fearful symmetry?

Jerusalem

And did those feet in ancient time
Walk upon England's mountains green?
And was the holy Lamb of God
On England's pleasant pastures seen?

And did the Countenance Divine
Shine forth upon our clouded hills?
And was Jerusalem builded here
Among these dark Satanic Mills?

Bring me my Bow of burning gold!
Bring me my Arrows of desire!
Bring me my Spear! O clouds, unfold!
Bring me my Chariot of fire!

I will not cease from Mental Fight,
Nor shall my Sword sleep in my hand,
Till we have built Jerusalem
In England's green and pleasant land.

Auguries of Innocence

To see a World in a Grain of Sand
And a Heaven in a Wild Flower,

Hold Infinity in the palm of your hand
And Eternity in an hour.

A Robin Red breast in a Cage
Puts all Heaven in a Rage,
A dove house fill'd with doves & Pigeons
Shudders Hell thro' all its regions.
A dog starv'd at his Master's Gate
Predicts the ruin of the State.
A Horse misus'd upon the Road
Calls to Heaven for Human blood.
Each outcry of the hunted Hare
A fibre from the Brain does tear.
A Skylark wounded in the wing,
A Cherubim does cease to sing.
The Game Cock clip'd & arm'd for fight
Does the Rising Sun affright.
Every Wolf's & Lion's howl
Raises from Hell a Human Soul.
The wild deer, wand'ring here & there,
Keeps the Human Soul from Care.
The Lamb misus'd breeds Public strife
And yet forgives the Butcher's Knife.
The Bat that flits at close of Eve
Has left the Brain that won't Believe.
The Owl that calls upon the Night
Speaks the Unbeliever's fright.
He who shall hurt the little Wren
Shall never be belov'd by Men.
He who the Ox to wrath has mov'd
Shall never be by Woman lov'd.
The wanton Boy that kills the Fly
Shall feel the Spider's enmity.
He who torments the Chafer's sprite
Weaves a Bower in endless Night.
The Catterpiller on the Leaf
Repeats to thee thy Mother's grief.
Kill not the Moth nor Butterfly,
For the Last Judgment draweth nigh.
He who shall train the Horse to War
Shall never pass the Polar Bar.

The Begger's Dog & Widow's Cat
Feed them & thou wilt grow fat.
The Gnat that sings his Summer's song
Poison gets from Slander's tongue.
The poison of the Snake & Newt
Is the sweat of Envy's Foot.
The Poison of the Honey Bee
Is the Artist's Jealousy.
The Prince's Robes & Beggar's Rags
Are Toadstools on the Miser's Bags.
A truth that's told with bad intent
Beats all the Lies you can invent.
It is right it should be so;
Man was made for Joy & Woe;
And when this we rightly know
Thro' the World we safely go.
Joy & Woe are woven fine,
A Clothing for the Soul divine;
Under every grief & pine
Runs a joy with silken twine.
The Babe is more than swadling Bands;
Throughout all these Human Lands
Tools were made, & Born were hands,
Every Farmer Understands.
Every Tear from Every Eye
Becomes a Babe in Eternity;
This is caught by Females bright
And return'd to its own delight.
The Bleat, the Bark, Bellow & Roar
Are Waves that Beat on Heaven's Shore.
The Babe that weeps the Rod beneath
Writes Revenge in realms of death.
The Beggar's Rags, fluttering in Air,
Does to Rags the Heaven tear.
The Soldier, arm'd with Sword & Gun,
Palsied strikes the Summer's Sun.
The poor Man's Farthing is worth more
Than all the Gold on Afric's Shore.
One Mite wrung from the Labrer's hands
Shall buy & sell the Miser's Lands:
Or, if protected from on high,

Does that whole Nation sell & buy.
He who mocks the Infant's Faith
Shall be mock'd in Age & Death.
He who shall teach the Child to Doubt
The rotting Grave shall ne'er get out.
He who respects the Infant's faith
Triumphs over Hell & Death.
The Child's Toys & the Old Man's Reasons
Are the Fruits of the Two seasons.
The Questioner, who sits so sly,
Shall never know how to Reply.
He who replies to words of Doubt
Doth put the Light of Knowledge out.
The Strongest Poison ever known
Came from Cæsar's Laurel Crown.
Nought can deform the Human Race
Like to the Armour's iron brace.
When Gold & Gems adorn the Plow
To peaceful Arts shall Envy Bow.
A Riddle or the Cricket's Cry
Is to Doubt a fit Reply.
The Emmet's Inch & Eagle's Mile
Make Lame Philosophy to smile.
He who Doubts from what he sees
Will ne'er Believe, do what you Please.
If the Sun & Moon should doubt,
They'd immediately Go out.
To be in a Passion you Good may do,
But no Good if a Passion is in you.
The Whore & Gambler, by the State
Licenc'd, build that Nation's Fate.
The Harlot's cry from Street to Street
Shall weave Old England's winding Sheet.
The Winner's Shout, the Loser's Curse,
Dance before dead England's Hearse.
Every Night & every Morn
Some to Misery are Born.
Every Morn & every Night
Some are Born to sweet delight.
Some are Born to sweet delight,
Some are Born to Endless Night.

We are led to Believe a Lie
When we see not Thro' the Eye
Which was Born in a Night to perish in a Night
When the Soul Slept in Beams of Light.
God Appears & God is Light
To those poor Souls who dwell in Night,
But does a Human Form Display
To those who Dwell in Realms of day.

ROBERT BURNS

Scots Wha Hae

Scots, wha hae wi' Wallace bled,
Scots, wham Bruce has aften led,
Welcome to your gory bed,
    Or to victory!

Now's the day, and now's the hour;
See the front o' battle lour,
See approach proud Edward's power –
    Chains and slavery!

Wha will be a traitor knave?
Wha can fill a coward's grave?
Wha sae base as be a slave? –
    Let him turn, and flee!

Wha for Scotland's King and Law
Freedom's sword will strongly draw,
Freeman stand or freeman fa',
    Let him follow me!

By Oppression's woes and pains,
By your sons in servile chains,
We will drain our dearest veins,
    But they shall be free!

Lay the proud usurpers low!
Tyrants fall in every foe!
Liberty's in every blow!
    Let us do, or die!

For A' That

Is there, for honest poverty,
  That hings his head, an' a' that?
The coward slave, we pass him by,
  We dare be poor for a' that!
    For a' that, an' a' that,
      Our toils obscure, an' a' that;
      The rank is but the guinea's stamp;
      The man's the gowd for a' that.

What though on hamely fare we dine,
  Wear hodden-gray, an' a' that;
Gie fools their silks, and knaves their wine,
  A man's a man for a' that.
    For a' that, an' a' that,
      Their tinsel show, an' a' that;
      The honest man, tho' e'er sae poor,
      Is king o' men for a' that.

Ye see yon birkie, ca'd a lord,
  Wha struts, an' stares, an' a' that;
Tho' hundreds worship at his word,
  He's but a cuif for a' that:
    For a' that, an' a that,
      His riband, star, an' a' that,
      The man o' independent mind,
      He looks and laughs at a' that.

A prince can mak a belted knight,
  A marquis, duke, an' a' that;
But an honest man's aboon his might,
  Guid faith, he mauna fa that!
    For a' that, an' a' that,
      Their dignities, an' a' that,
      The pith o' sense, an' pride o' worth,
      Are higher rank than a' that.

Then let us pray that come it may
  (As come it will for a' that)
That Sense and Worth o'er a' the earth,
  Shall bear the gree and a' that!

For a' that, and a' that,
   It's coming yet, for a' that,
That man to man the world o'er
   Shall brithers be for a' that.

SAMUEL ROGERS

A Wish

Mine be a cot beside the hill;
   A bee-hive's hum shall soothe my ear;
A willowy brook, that turns a mill,
   With many a fall shall linger near.

The swallow oft beneath my thatch
   Shall twitter from her clay-built nest;
Oft shall the pilgrim lift the latch
   And share my meal, a welcome guest.

Around my ivied porch shall spring
   Each fragrant flower that drinks the dew;
And Lucy at her wheel shall sing
   In russet gown and apron blue.

The village church among the trees,
   Where first our marriage vows were given,
With merry peals shall swell the breeze
   And point with taper spire to Heaven.

JAMES HOGG

A Boy's Song

Where the pools are bright and deep,
Where the gray trout lies asleep,
Up the river and o'er the lea,
That's the way for Billy and me.

Where the blackbird sings the latest,
Where the hawthorn blooms the sweetest,
Where the nestlings chirp and flee,
That's the way for Billy and me.

Where the mowers mow the cleanest,
Where the hay lies thick and greenest;
There to trace the homeward bee,
That's the way for Billy and me.

Where the hazel bank is steepest,
Where the shadow falls the deepest,
Where the clustering nuts fall free,
That's the way for Billy and me.

Why the boys should drive away
Little sweet maidens from the play,
Or love to banter and fight so well,
That's the thing I never could tell.

But this I know, I love to play,
Through the meadow, among the hay;
Up the water and o'er the lea,
That's the way for Billy and me.

WILLIAM WORDSWORTH

The World Is Too Much with Us

The world is too much with us; late and soon,
Getting and spending, we lay waste our powers:
Little we see in Nature that is ours;
We have given our hearts away, a sordid boon!
This Sea that bares her bosom to the moon;
The Winds that will be howling at all hours
And are up-gathered now like sleeping flowers;
For this, for every thing, we are out of tune;
It moves us not. – Great God! I'd rather be
A Pagan suckled in a creed outworn;
So might I, standing on this pleasant lea,

Have glimpses that would make me less forlorn;
Have sight of Proteus rising from the sea;
Or hear old Triton blow his wreathed horn.

Milton!

Milton! thou should'st be living at this hour:
England hath need of thee: she is a fen
Of stagnant waters: altar, sword and pen,
Fireside, the heroic wealth of hall and bower,
Have forfeited their ancient English dower
Of inward happiness. We are selfish men;
Oh! raise us up, return to us again;
And give us manners, virtue, freedom, power.
Thy soul was like a Star, and dwelt apart:
Thou hadst a voice whose sound was like the sea:
Pure as the naked heavens, majestic, free,
So didst thou travel on life's common way,
In cheerful godliness; and yet thy heart
The lowliest duties on itself did lay.

We Must Be Free or Die

It is not to be thought of that the Flood
    Of British freedom, which, to the open sea
    Of the world's praise, from dark antiquity
Hath flowed, 'with pomp of waters, unwithstood', –
Roused though it be full often to a mood
    Which spurns the check of salutary bands, –
    That this most famous Stream in bogs and sands
Should perish; and to evil and to good
Be lost for ever. In our halls is hung
    Armoury of the invincible Knights of old:
We must be free or die, who speak the tongue
    That Shakespeare spake; the faith and morals hold
Which Milton held. – In every thing we are sprung
    Of Earth's first blood, have titles manifold.

Upon Westminster Bridge

Earth has not anything to show more fair:
   Dull would he be of soul who could pass by
   A sight so touching in its majesty:
This City now doth, like a garment, wear
The beauty of the morning; silent, bare,
   Ships, towers, domes, theatres, and temples lie
   Open unto the fields, and to the sky;
All bright and glittering in the smokeless air.
Never did sun more beautifully steep
   In his first splendour, valley, rock, or hill;
Ne'er saw I, never felt, a calm so deep!
   The river glideth at his own sweet will:
Dear God! the very houses seem asleep;
   And all that mighty heart is lying still!

The Solitary Reaper

Behold her, single in the field,
   Yon solitary Highland Lass!
Reaping and singing by herself;
   Stop here, or gently pass!
Alone she cuts and binds the grain,
And sings a melancholy strain;
O listen! for the vale profound
Is overflowing with the sound.

No nightingale did ever chaunt
   More welcome notes to weary bands
Of travellers in some shady haunt,
   Among Arabian sands:
A voice so thrilling ne'er was heard
In spring-time from the cuckoo-bird,
Breaking the silence of the seas
Among the farthest Hebrides.

Will no one tell me what she sings? –
   Perhaps the plaintive numbers flow

For old, unhappy, far-off things,
    And battles long ago:
Or is it some more humble lay,
Familiar matter of to-day?
Some natural sorrow, loss, or pain,
That has been, and may be again?

Whate'er the theme, the maiden sang
    As if her song could have no ending;
I saw her singing at her work,
    And o'er the sickle bending; –
I listened, motionless and still;
And, as I mounted up the hill,
The music in my heart I bore,
Long after it was heard no more.

SIR WALTER SCOTT

The Patriot

Breathes there the man, with soul so dead,
Who never to himself hath said,
    This is my own, my native land!
Whose heart hath ne'er within him burned,
As home his footsteps he hath turned,
    From wandering on a foreign strand!
If such there breathe, go, mark him well;
For him no Minstrel raptures swell;
High though his titles, proud his name,
Boundless his wealth as wish can claim;
Despite those titles, power, and pelf,
The wretch, concentred all in self,
Living, shall forfeit fair renown,
And, doubly, dying, shall go down
To the vile dust, from whence he sprung,
Unwept, unhonoured, and unsung.

*

O Caledonia! stern and wild,
Meet nurse for a poetic child!

72

Land of brown heath and shaggy wood,
Land of the mountain and the flood,
Land of my sires! what mortal hand
Can e'er untie the filial band,
That knits me to thy rugged strand!
Still, as I view each well known scene,
Think what is now, and what hath been,
Seems as, to me, of all bereft,
Sole friends thy woods and streams were left;
And thus I love them better still,
Even in extremity of ill.
By Yarrow's stream still let me stray,
Though none should guide my feeble way;
Still feel the breeze down Ettricke break,
Although it chill my withered cheek;
Still lay my head by Teviot Stone,
Though there, forgotten and alone,
The Bard may draw his parting groan.

Pibroch

Pibroch of Donuil Dhu,
   Pibroch of Donuil,
Wake thy wild voice anew,
   Summon Clan-Conuil.
Come away, come away,
   Hark to the summons!
Come in your war array,
   Gentles and commons.

Come from deep glen and
   From mountain so rocky,
The war-pipe and pennon
   Are at Inverlocky.
Come every hill-plaid and
   True heart that wears one,
Come every steel blade and
   Strong hand that bears one.

Leave untended the herd,
  The flock without shelter;
Leave the corpse uninterred,
  The bride at the altar;
Leave the deer, leave the steer,
  Leave nets and barges;
Come with your fighting gear,
  Broadswords and targes.

Come as the winds come when
  Forests are rended,
Come as the waves come when
  Navies are stranded:
Faster come, faster come,
  Faster and faster,
Chief, vassal, page and groom,
  Tenant and master.

Fast they come, fast they come;
  See how they gather!
Wide waves the eagle plume
  Blended with heather.
Cast your plaids, draw your blades,
  Forward each man set!
Pibroch of Donuil Dhu,
  Knell for the onset!

ROBERT SOUTHEY

The Battle of Blenheim

It was a summer evening,
  Old Kaspar's work was done,
And he before his cottage door
  Was sitting in the sun,
And by him sported on the green
His little grandchild Wilhelmine.

She saw her brother Peterkin
  Roll something large and round,

Which he beside the rivulet
  In playing there had found;
He came to ask what he had found,
That was so large, and smooth, and round.

Old Kaspar took it from the boy,
  Who stood expectant by;
And then the old man shook his head,
  And with a natural sigh,
'Tis some poor fellow's skull, said he,
Who fell in the great victory.

I find them in the garden,
  For there's many here about,
And often when I go to plough,
  The ploughshare turns them out;
For many thousand men, said he,
Were slain in the great victory.

Now tell us what 'twas all about,
  Young Peterkin, he cries,
And little Wilhelmine looks up
  With wonder-waiting eyes;
Now tell us all about the war,
And what they kill'd each other for.

It was the English, Kaspar cried,
  That put the French to rout;
But what they kill'd each other for,
  I could not well make out;
But every body said, quoth he,
That 'twas a famous victory.

My father lived at Blenheim then,
  Yon little stream hard by;
They burnt his dwelling to the ground
  And he was forced to fly;
So with his wife and child he fled,
Nor had he where to rest his head.

With fire and sword the country round
  Was wasted far and wide,

And many a childing mother then,
  And new-born baby died.
But things like that, you know, must be
At every famous victory.

They say it was a shocking sight
  After the field was won,
For many thousand bodies here
  Lay rotting in the sun;
But things like that, you know, must be
After a famous victory.

Great praise the Duke of Marlbro' won,
  And our good Prince Eugene. –
Why 'twas a very wicked thing!
  Said little Wilhelmine.
Nay – nay – my little girl, quoth he,
It was a famous victory.

And every body praised the Duke
  Who this great fight did win.
But what good came of it at last?
  Quoth little Peterkin.
Why that I cannot tell, said he,
But 'twas a famous victory.

CHARLES LAMB

The Old Familiar Faces

I have had playmates, I have had companions,
In my days of childhood, in my joyful school-days,
All, all are gone, the old familiar faces.

I have been laughing, I have been carousing,
Drinking late, sitting late, with my bosom cronies,
All, all are gone, the old familiar faces.

I loved a love once, fairest among women:
Closed are her doors on me, I must not see her –
All, all are gone, the old familiar faces.

I have a friend, a kinder friend has no man;
Like an ingrate, I left my friend abruptly;
Left him, to muse on the old familiar faces.

Ghost-like I paced round the haunts of my childhood,
Earth seemed a desert I was bound to traverse,
Seeking to find the old familiar faces.

Friend of my bosom, thou more than a brother,
Why wert not thou born in my father's dwelling?
So might we talk of the old familiar faces –

How some they have died, and some they have left me,
And some are taken from me; all are departed;
All, all are gone, the old familiar faces.

W. S. LANDOR

I Strove with None

I strove with none, for none was worth my strife:
    Nature I loved, and next to Nature, Art:
I warm'd both hands before the fire of Life;
    It sinks; and I am ready to depart.

THOMAS CAMPBELL

The Battle of the Baltic

Of Nelson and the North
Sing the glorious day's renown,
When to battle fierce came forth
All the might of Denmark's crown,
And her arms along the deep proudly shone;
By each gun the lighted brand
In a bold determined hand,
And the Prince of all the land
Led them on.

77

Like leviathans afloat,
Lay their bulwarks on the brine;
While the sign of battle flew
On the lofty British line:
It was ten of April morn by the chime:
As they drifted on their path,
There was silence deep as death;
And the boldest held his breath,
For a time.

But the might of England flushed
To anticipate the scene;
And her van the fleeter rushed
O'er the deadly space between.
'Hearts of oak!' our captains cried; when each gun
From its adamantine lips
Spread a death-shade round the ships,
Like the hurricane eclipse
Of the sun.

Again! again! again!
And the havoc did not slack,
Till a feeble cheer the Dane,
To our cheering sent us back; –
Their shots along the deep slowly boom: –
Then ceased – and all is wail,
As they strike the shattered sail;
Or, in conflagration pale
Light the gloom.

Now joy, Old England, raise
For the tidings of thy might,
By the festal cities' blaze,
Whilst the wine-cup shines in light;
And yet amidst that joy and uproar,
Let us think of them that sleep
Full many a fathom deep
By thy wild and stormy steep,
Elsinore!

Lord Ullin's Daughter

A chieftain to the Highlands bound
Cries 'Boatman, do not tarry!
And I'll give thee a silver pound
To row us o'er the ferry!'

'Now who be ye, would cross Lochgyle
This dark and stormy water?'
'O I'm the chief of Ulva's isle,
And this, Lord Ullin's daughter.

'And fast before her father's men
Three days we've fled together,
For should he find us in the glen,
My blood would stain the heather.

'His horsemen hard behind us ride –
Should they our steps discover,
Then who will cheer my bonny bride
When they have slain her lover?'

Out spoke the hardy Highland wight,
'I'll go, my chief, I'm ready:
It is not for your silver bright,
But for your winsome lady: –

'And by my word! the bonny bird
In danger shall not tarry;
So though the waves are raging white
I'll row you o'er the ferry.'

By this the storm grew loud apace,
The water-wraith was shrieking;
And in the scowl of heaven each face
Grew dark as they were speaking.

But still as wilder blew the wind
And as the night grew drearer,
Adown the glen rode armèd men,
Their trampling sounded nearer.

'O haste thee, haste!' the lady cries,
'Though tempests round us gather;
I'll meet the raging of the skies,
But not an angry father.'

The boat has left a stormy land,
A stormy sea before her, –
When, O! too strong for human hand
The tempest gather'd o'er her.

And still they row'd amidst the roar
Of waters fast prevailing:
Lord Ullin reach'd that fatal shore, –
His wrath was changed to wailing.

For, sore dismay'd, through storm and shade
His child he did discover:–
One lovely hand she stretch'd for aid,
And one was round her lover.

'Come back! come back!' he cried in grief
'Across this stormy water:
And I'll forgive your Highland chief,
My daughter! – O my daughter!'

'Twas vain: the loud waves lash'd the shore,
Return or aid preventing:
The waters wild went o'er his child,
And he was left lamenting.

The Soldier's Dream

Our bugles sang truce, for the night-cloud had lower'd,
  And the sentinel stars set their watch in the sky;
And thousands had sunk on the ground overpower'd,
  The weary to sleep, and the wounded to die.

When reposing that night on my pallet of straw
  By the wolf-scaring faggot that guarded the slain,

At the dead of the night a sweet Vision I saw;
  And thrice ere the morning I dreamt it again.

Methought from the battle-field's dreadful array
  Far, far, I had roam'd on a desolate track:
'Twas Autumn, – and sunshine arose on the way
  To the home of my fathers, that welcomed me back.

I flew to the pleasant fields traversed so oft
  In life's morning march, when my bosom was young;
I heard my own mountain-goats bleating aloft,
  And knew the sweet strain that the corn-reapers sung.

Then pledged me the wine-cup, and fondly I swore
  From my home and my weeping friends never to part;
My little ones kiss'd me a thousand times o'er,
  And my wife sobb'd aloud in her fullness of heart.

'Stay – stay with us! – rest! – thou art weary and worn!' –
  And fain was their war-broken soldier to stay; –
But sorrow return'd with the dawning of morn,
  And the voice in my dreaming ear melted away.

Hohenlinden

On Linden, when the sun was low,
All bloodless lay the untrodden snow,
And dark as winter was the flow
    Of Iser, rolling rapidly.

But Linden saw another sight,
When the drum beat, at dead of night,
Commanding fires of death to light
    The darkness of her scenery.

By torch and trumpet fast array'd,
Each horseman drew his battle blade,
And furious every charger neigh'd
    To join the dreadful revelry.

Then shook the hills, with thunder riven;
Then rushed the steed, to battle driven;
And, louder than the bolt of heaven,
 Far flash'd the red artillery.

But redder yet that light shall glow,
On Linden's hills of stained snow;
And bloodier yet, the torrent flow
 Of Iser, rolling rapidly.

'Tis morn; but scarce yon level sun
Can pierce the war-clouds, rolling dun,
Where furious Frank, and fiery Hun,
 Shout in their sulph'rous canopy.

The combat deepens. On, ye brave,
Who rush to glory, or the grave!
Wave, Munich, all thy banners wave,
 And charge with all thy chivalry!

Few, few, shall part, where many meet!
The snow shall be their winding sheet,
And every turf, beneath their feet,
 Shall be a soldier's sepulchre.

Ye Mariners of England

Ye Mariners of England
 That guard our native seas!
Whose flag has braved a thousand years
 The battle and the breeze!
Your glorious standard launch again
 To match another foe;
And sweep through the deep,
 While the stormy winds do blow!
While the battle rages loud and long
 And the stormy winds do blow.

The spirits of your fathers
 Shall start from every wave –

For the deck it was their field of fame,
    And Ocean was their grave:
Where Blake and mighty Nelson fell
    Your manly hearts shall glow,
As ye sweep through the deep,
    While the stormy winds do blow!
While the battle rages loud and long
    And the stormy winds do blow.

Britannia needs no bulwarks,
    No towers along the steep;
Her march is o'er the mountain-waves,
    Her home is on the deep.
With thunders from her native oak
    She quells the floods below,
As they roar on the shore,
    When the stormy winds do blow!
When the battle rages loud and long,
    And the stormy winds do blow.

The meteor flag of England
    Shall yet terrific burn;
Till danger's troubled night depart
    And the star of peace return.
Then, then, ye ocean-warriors!
    Our song and feast shall flow
To the fame of your name,
    When the storm has ceased to blow!
When the fiery fight is heard no more,
    And the storm has ceased to blow.

JOHN GALT (attrib.)

Canadian Boat-song

Listen to me, as when ye heard our father
    Sing long ago the song of other shores –
Listen to me, and then in chorus gather
    All your deep voices, as ye pull your oars:

> *Fair these broad meads – these hoary woods are grand;*
> *But we are exiles from our fathers' land.*

From the lone shieling of the misty island
  Mountains divide us, and the waste of seas –
Yet still the blood is strong, the heart is Highland,
  And we in dreams behold the Hebrides:
    Fair these broad meads, etc.

We ne'er shall tread the fancy-haunted valley,
  Where 'tween the dark hills creeps the small clear **stream**,
In arms around the patriarch banner rally,
  Nor see the moon on royal tombstones gleam:
    Fair these broad meads, etc.

When the bold kindred, in the time long-vanish'd,
  Conquer'd the soil and fortified the keep, –
No seer foretold the children would be banish'd,
  That a degenerate Lord might boast his sheep:
    Fair these broad meads, etc.

Come foreign rage – let Discord burst in slaughter!
  O then for clansman true, and stern claymore –
The hearts that would have given their blood like water,
  Beat heavily beyond the Atlantic roar:
    Fair these broad meads – these hoary woods are grand;
    But we are exiles from our fathers' land.

FRANCIS SCOTT KEY

The Star-Spangled Banner

O say, can you see, by the dawn's early light,
  What so proudly we hailed at the twilight's last gleaming –
Whose broad stripes and bright stars, through the clouds of the
    fight,
  O'er the ramparts we watched were so gallantly streaming!

And the rocket's red glare, the bombs bursting in air,
Gave proof through the night that our flag was still there;
O! say, does that star-spangled banner yet wave
O'er the land of the free, and the home of the brave?

On that shore dimly seen through the mists of the deep,
    Where the foe's haughty host in dread silence reposes,
What is that which the breeze, o'er the towering steep,
    As it fitfully blows, now conceals, now discloses?
Now it catches the gleam of the morning's first beam,
In full glory reflected now shines on the stream;
'Tis the star-spangled banner; O long may it wave
O'er the land of the free, and the home of the brave!

And where is that band who so vauntingly swore
    That the havoc of war and the battle's confusion
A home and a country should leave us no more?
    Their blood has washed out their foul footsteps' pollution.
No refuge could save the hireling and slave
From the terror of flight, or the gloom of the grave;
And the star-spangled banner in triumph doth wave
O'er the land of the free, and the home of the brave.

O! thus be it ever, when freemen shall stand
    Between their loved homes and the war's desolation!
Blest with victory and peace, may the heav'n-rescued land
    Praise the power that hath made and preserved us a nation.
Then conquer we must, when our cause it is just,
And this be our motto – '*In God is our trust*':
And the star-spangled banner in triumph shall wave
O'er the land of the free, and the home of the brave.

THOMAS MOORE

The Harp that once through Tara's Halls

The harp that once through Tara's halls,
    The soul of music shed,
Now hangs as mute on Tara's walls
    As if that soul were fled. –

So sleeps the pride of former days,
    So glory's thrill is o'er,
And hearts, that once beat high for praise,
    Now feel that pulse no more!

No more to chiefs and ladies bright
    The harp of Tara swells:
The chord, alone, that breaks at night,
    Its tale of ruin tells.
Thus Freedom now so seldom wakes,
    The only throb she gives,
Is when some heart indignant breaks,
    To shew that still she lives!

REGINALD HEBER

From Greenland's Icy Mountains

From Greenland's icy mountains,
    From India's coral strand,
Where Afric's sunny fountains
    Roll down their golden sand,
From many an ancient river,
    From many a palmy plain,
They call us to deliver
    Their land from error's chain.

What though the spicy breezes
    Blow soft o'er Java's isle,
Though every prospect pleases
    And only man is vile,
In vain with lavish kindness
    The gifts of God are strown,
The heathen in his blindness
    Bows down to wood and stone.

Can we, whose souls are lighted
    With wisdom from on high,
Can we to men benighted
    The lamp of life deny?

Salvation! oh, salvation!
    The joyful sound proclaim,
Till each remotest nation
    Has learned Messiah's name.

Waft, waft, ye winds, his story,
    And you, ye waters, roll,
Till, like a sea of glory,
    It spreads from pole to pole;
Till o'er our ransomed nature
    The Lamb for sinners slain,
Redeemer, King, Creator,
    In bliss returns to reign.

ALLAN CUNNINGHAM

A Sea-song

A wet sheet and a flowing sea,
    A wind that follows fast
And fills the white and rustling sail
    And bends the gallant mast;
And bends the gallant mast, my boys,
    While like the eagle free
Away the good ship flies, and leaves
    Old England on the lee.

O for a soft and gentle wind!
    I heard a fair one cry:
But give to me the snoring breeze
    And white waves heaving high;
And white waves heaving high, my lads,
    The good ship tight and free –
The world of waters is our home,
    And merry men are we.

There's tempest in yon hornèd moon,
    And lightning in yon cloud;
But hark the music, mariners!
    The wind is piping loud;

The wind is piping loud, my boys,
    The lightning flashes free -
While the hollow oak our palace is,
    Our heritage the sea.

LEIGH HUNT

Abou Ben Adhem

Abou Ben Adhem (may his tribe increase!)
Awoke one night from a deep dream of peace,
And saw, within the moonlight in his room,
Making it rich, and like a lily in bloom,
An angel writing in a book of gold: –
Exceeding peace had made Ben Adhem bold,
And to the presence in the room he said,
   'What writest thou?' – The vision raised its head,
And with a look made of all sweet accord,
Answered, 'The names of those who love the Lord.'
'And is mine one?' said Abou. 'Nay, not so,'
Replied the angel. Abou spoke more low,
But cheerly still; and said, 'I pray thee, then,
Write me as one that loves his fellow men.'
   The angel wrote, and vanished. The next night
It came again with a great wakening light,
And showed the names whom love of God had blest,
And lo! Ben Adhem's name led all the rest.

THOMAS LOVE PEACOCK

The War Song of Dinas Vawr

The mountain sheep are sweeter,
But the valley sheep are fatter;
We therefore deemed it meeter
To carry off the latter.
We made an expedition;
We met a host, and quelled it;
We forced a strong position,
And killed the men who held it.

On Dyfed's richest valley,
Where herds of kine were brousing,
We made a mighty sally,
To furnish our carousing.
Fierce warriors rushed to meet us;
We met them, and o'erthrew them:
They struggled hard to beat us;
But we conquered them, and slew them.

As we drove our prize at leisure,
The king marched forth to catch us:
His rage surpassed all measure,
But his people could not match us.
He fled to his hall-pillars;
And, ere our force we led off,
Some sacked his house and cellars,
While others cut his head off.

We there, in strife bewildering,
Spilt blood enough to swim in:
We orphaned many children,
And widowed many women.
The eagles and the ravens
We glutted with our foemen;
The heroes and the cravens,
The spearmen and the bowmen.

We brought away from battle,
And much their land bemoaned them,
Two thousand head of cattle,
And the head of him who owned them:
Ednyfed, king of Dyfed,
His head was borne before us;
His wine and beasts supplied our feasts,
And his overthrow, our chorus.

LORD BYRON

The Destruction of Sennacherib

The Assyrian came down like the wolf on the fold,
And his cohorts were gleaming in purple and gold;
And the sheen of their spears was like stars on the sea,
When the blue wave rolls nightly on deep Galilee.

Like the leaves of the forest when Summer is green,
That host with their banners at sunset were seen:
Like the leaves of the forest when Autumn hath blown,
That host on the morrow lay withered and strown.

For the Angel of Death spread his wings on the blast,
And breathed in the face of the foe as he passed;
And the eyes of the sleepers waxed deadly and chill,
And their hearts but once heaved, and for ever grew still!

And there lay the steed with his nostril all wide,
But through it there rolled not the breath of his pride:
And the foam of his gasping lay white on the turf,
And cold as the spray of the rock-beating surf.

And there lay the rider distorted and pale,
With the dew on his brow and the rust on his mail;
And the tents were all silent, the banners alone,
The lances unlifted, the trumpet unblown.

And the widows of Ashur are loud in their wail,
And the idols are broke in the temple of Baal;
And the might of the Gentile, unsmote by the sword,
Hath melted like snow in the glance of the Lord!

The Isles of Greece

The isles of Greece! the isles of Greece
  Where burning Sappho loved and sung,
Where grew the arts of war and peace,
  Where Delos rose, and Phœbus sprung!

Eternal summer gilds them yet,
But all, except their sun, is set.

The Scian and the Teian muse,
    The hero's harp, the lover's lute,
Have found the fame your shores refuse:
    Their place of birth alone is mute
To sounds which echo further west
Than your sires' 'Islands of the Blest.'

The mountains look on Marathon –
    And Marathon looks on the sea;
And musing there an hour alone,
    I dreamed that Greece might still be free;
For standing on the Persians' grave,
I could not deem myself a slave.

A king sate on the rocky brow
    Which looks o'er sea-born Salamis;
And ships, by thousands, lay below,
    And men in nations; – all were his!
He counted them at break of day –
And when the sun set, where were they?

And where are they? and where art thou,
    My country? On thy voiceless shore
The heroic lay is tuneless now –
    The heroic bosom beats no more!
And must thy lyre, so long divine,
Degenerate into hands like mine?

'Tis something in the dearth of fame,
    Though linked among a fettered race,
To feel at least a patriot's shame,
    Even as I sing, suffuse my face;
For what is left the poet here?
For Greeks a blush – for Greece a tear.

Must *we* but weep o'er days more blest?
    Must *we* but blush? – Our fathers bled.
Earth! render back from out thy breast
    A remnant of our Spartan dead!

Of the three hundred grant but three,
To make a new Thermopylæ!

What, silent still? and silent all?
    Ah! no; – the voices of the dead
Sound like a distant torrent's fall,
    And answer, 'Let one living head,
But one, arise, – we come, we come!'
'Tis but the living who are dumb.

In vain – in vain: strike other chords;
    Fill high the cup with Samian wine!
Leave battles to the Turkish hordes,
    And shed the blood of Scio's vine!
Hark! rising to the ignoble call –
How answers each bold Bacchanal!

You have the Pyrrhic dance as yet;
    Where is the Pyrrhic phalanx gone?
Of two such lessons, why forget
    The nobler and the manlier one?
You have the letters Cadmus gave –
Think ye he meant them for a slave?

Fill high the bowl with Samian wine!
    We will not think of themes like these!
It made Anacreon's song divine:
    He served – but served Polycrates –
A tyrant; but our masters then
Were still, at least, our countrymen.

The tyrant of the Chersonese
    Was freedom's best and bravest friend;
That tyrant was Miltiades!
    O that the present hour would lend
Another despot of the kind!
Such chains as his were sure to bind.

Fill high the bowl with Samian wine!
    On Suli's rock, and Parga's shore,
Exists the remnant of a line
    Such as the Doric mothers bore;

And there, perhaps, some seed is sown,
The Heracleidan blood might own.

Trust not for freedom to the Franks –
   They have a king who buys and sells;
In native swords and native ranks
   The only hope of courage dwells:
But Turkish force and Latin fraud
Would break your shield, however broad.

Fill high the bowl with Samian wine!
   Our virgins dance beneath the shade –
I see their glorious black eyes shine;
   But gazing on each glowing maid,
My own the burning tear-drop laves,
To think such breasts must suckle slaves.

Place me on Sunium's marbled steep,
   Where nothing, save the waves and I,
May hear our mutual murmurs sweep;
   There, swan-like, let me sing and die:
A land of slaves shall ne'er be mine –
Dash down yon cup of Samian wine!

We'll Go No More a Roving

So, we'll go no more a roving
   So late into the night,
Though the heart be still as loving,
   And the moon be still as bright.

For the sword outwears its sheath,
   And the soul wears out the breast,
And the heart must pause to breathe,
   And love itself have rest.

Though the night was made for loving,
   And the day returns too soon,
Yet we'll go no more a roving
   By the light of the moon.

CHARLES WOLFE

The Burial of Sir John Moore after Corunna

Not a drum was heard, not a funeral note,
   As his corpse to the rampart we hurried;
Not a soldier discharged his farewell shot
   O'er the grave where our hero we buried.

We buried him darkly at dead of night,
   The sods with our bayonets turning,
By the struggling moonbeam's misty light
   And the lanthorn dimly burning.

No useless coffin enclosed his breast,
   Not in sheet or in shroud we wound him;
But he lay like a warrior taking his rest
   With his martial cloak around him.

Few and short were the prayers we said,
   And we spoke not a word of sorrow;
But we steadfastly gazed on the face that was dead,
   And we bitterly thought of the morrow.

We thought, as we hollowed his narrow bed
   And smoothed down his lonely pillow,
That the foe and the stranger would tread o'er his head,
   And we far away on the billow!

Lightly they'll talk of the spirit that's gone,
   And o'er his cold ashes upbraid him –
But little he'll reck, if they let him sleep on
   In the grave where a Briton has laid him.

But half of our heavy task was done
   When the clock struck the hour for retiring;
And we heard the distant and random gun
   That the foe was sullenly firing.

Slowly and sadly we laid him down,
   From the field of his fame fresh and gory;
We carved not a line, and we raised not a stone,
   But we left him alone with his glory.

JOHN KEBLE

New Every Morning

New every morning is the love
Our wakening and uprising prove;
Through sleep and darkness safely brought,
Restored to life, and power, and thought.

New mercies, each returning day,
Hover around us while we pray;
New perils past, new sins forgiven,
New thoughts of God, new hopes of heaven.

If on our daily course our mind
Be set to hallow all we find,
New treasures still, of countless price,
God will provide for sacrifice.

Old friends, old scenes, will lovelier be,
As more of heaven in each we see;
Some softening gleam of love and prayer
Shall dawn on every cross and care.

We need not bid, for cloistered cell,
Our neighbour and our work farewell,
Nor strive to wind ourselves too high
For sinful man beneath the sky:

The trivial round, the common task,
Would furnish all we ought to ask, –
Room to deny ourselves, a road
To bring us daily nearer God.

Only, O Lord, in thy dear love
Fit us for perfect rest above;
And help us this and every day
To live more nearly as we pray.

P. B. SHELLEY

Ozymandias

I met a traveller from an antique land
Who said: Two vast and trunkless legs of stone
Stand in the desert. Near them, on the sand,
Half sunk, a shattered visage lies, whose frown,
And wrinkled lip, and sneer of cold command,
Tell that its sculptor well those passions read
Which yet survive, stamped on these lifeless things,
The hand that mocked them, and the heart that fed:
And on the pedestal these words appear:
'My name is Ozymandias, king of kings:
Look on my works, ye Mighty, and despair!'
Nothing beside remains. Round the decay
Of that colossal wreck, boundless and bare
The lone and level sands stretch far away.

FELICIA D. HEMANS

The Homes of England

The stately homes of England,
  How beautiful they stand
Amidst their tall ancestral trees,
  O'er all the pleasant land!
The deer across their greensward bound,
  Through shade and sunny gleam;
And the swan glides past them with the sound
  Of some rejoicing stream.

The merry homes of England!
  Around their hearths by night,
What gladsome looks of household love
  Meet in the ruddy light!
There woman's voice flows forth in song,
  Or childhood's tale is told,
Or lips move tunefully along
  Some glorious page of old.

The blessed homes of England!
  How softly on their bowers
Is laid the holy quietness
  That breathes from Sabbath hours!
Solemn, yet sweet, the church-bell's chime
  Floats through their woods at morn;
All other sounds, in that still time,
  Of breeze and leaf are born.

The cottage homes of England!
  By thousands on her plains,
They are smiling o'er the silvery brooks,
  And round the hamlet fanes.
Through glowing orchards forth they peep,
  Each from its nook of leaves;
And fearless there the lowly sleep,
  As the bird beneath their eaves.

The free fair homes of England!
  Long, long, in hut and hall,
May hearts of native proof be reared
  To guard each hallowed wall!
And green for ever be the groves,
  And bright the flowery sod,
Where first the child's glad spirit loves
  Its country and its God!

The Graves of a Household

They grew in beauty side by side,
  They filled one home with glee; –
Their graves are scattered far and wide,
  By mount, and stream, and sea.

The same fond mother bent at night
  O'er each fair sleeping brow:
She had each folded flower in sight –
  Where are those dreamers now?

One, 'midst the forest of the West,
    By a dark stream is laid –
The Indian knows his place of rest,
    Far in the cedar shade.

The sea, the blue lone sea, hath one –
    He lies where pearls lie deep,
He was the loved of all, yet none
    O'er his low bed may weep.

One sleeps where southern vines are drest
    Above the noble slain:
He wrapt his colours round his breast
    On a blood-red field of Spain.

And one – o'er *her* the myrtle showers
    Its leaves, by soft winds fanned;
She faded 'midst Italian flowers –
    The last of that bright band.

And parted thus they rest, who played
    Beneath the same green tree;
Whose voices mingled as they prayed
    Around one parent knee!

They that with smiles lit up the hall,
    And cheered with song the hearth! –
Alas, for love! if *thou* wert all,
    And nought beyond, O Earth!

H. F. LYTE

Abide with Me

Abide with me; fast falls the eventide;
The darkness deepens; Lord, with me abide.
When other helpers fail, and comforts flee,
Help of the helpless, O abide with me!

Swift to its close ebbs out life's little day;
Earth's joys grow dim, its glories pass away:
Change and decay in all around I see,
O Thou who changest not, abide with me.

Not a brief glance I beg, a passing word;
But as Thou dweltst with Thy disciples, Lord,
Familiar, condescending, patient, free, –
Come, not to sojourn, but abide with me.

Come not in terrors, as the King of kings;
But kind and good, with healing in Thy wings,
Tears for all woes, a heart for every plea,
Come, Friend of sinners, and thus bide with me.

Thou on my head in early youth didst smile,
And, though rebellious and perverse meanwhile,
Thou hast not left me, oft as I left Thee,
On to the close, O Lord, abide with me!

I need Thy presence every passing hour;
What but Thy grace can foil the tempter's power?
Who like Thyself my guide and stay can be?
Through cloud and sunshine, Lord, abide with me.

I fear no foe with Thee at hand to bless;
Ills have no weight and tears no bitterness;
Where is death's sting? Where, grave, thy victory?
I triumph still if Thou abide with me.

Hold Thou Thy cross before my closing eyes;
Shine through the gloom and point me to the skies!
Heaven's morning breaks and earth's vain shadows flee;
In life, in death, O Lord, abide with me.

THOMAS HOOD

The Song of the Shirt

With fingers weary and worn,
  With eyelids heavy and red,
A woman sat, in unwomanly rags,
  Plying her needle and thread –
Stitch! stitch! stitch!
  In poverty, hunger, and dirt,
And still with a voice of dolorous pitch
  She sang the 'Song of the Shirt.'

'Work! work! work!
  While the cock is crowing aloof!
And work – work – work,
  Till the stars shine through the roof!
It's Oh! to be a slave
  Along with the barbarous Turk,
Where woman has never a soul to save,
  If this is Christian work.

'Work – work – work,
  Till the brain begins to swim;
Work – work – work,
  Till the eyes are heavy and dim!
Seam, and gusset, and band,
  Band, and gusset, and seam,
Till over the buttons I fall asleep,
  And sew them on in a dream!

'Oh, Men, with Sisters dear!
  Oh, Men, with Mothers and Wives!
It is not linen you're wearing out
  But human creatures' lives!
Stitch – stitch – stitch,
  In poverty, hunger, and dirt,
Sewing at once, with a double thread,
  A Shroud as well as a Shirt.

'But why do I talk of Death?
   That Phantom of grisly bone,
I hardly fear its terrible shape,
   It seems so like my own –
It seems so like my own,
   Because of the fasts I keep;
Oh, God, that bread should be so dear,
   And flesh and blood so cheap!

'Work – work – work!
   My labour never flags;
And what are its wages? A bed of straw,
   A crust of bread – and rags.
That shattered roof – this naked floor –
   A table – a broken chair –
And a wall so blank, my shadow I thank
   For sometimes falling there!

'Work – work – work!
   From weary chime to chime,
Work – work – work,
   As prisoners work for crime!
Band, and gusset, and seam,
   Seam, and gusset, and band,
Till the heart is sick, and the brain benumbed,
   As well as the weary hand.

'Work – work – work!
   In the dull December light,
And work – work – work,
   When the weather is warm and bright –
While underneath the eaves
   The brooding swallows cling
As if to show me their sunny backs
   And twit me with the spring.

'Oh! but to breathe the breath
   Of the cowslip and primrose sweet –
With the sky above my head,
   And the grass beneath my feet;

For only one short hour
  To feel as I used to feel,
Before I knew the woes of want
  And the walk that costs a meal.

'Oh! but for one short hour!
  A respite however brief!
No blessèd leisure for Love or Hope,
  But only time for Grief!
A little weeping would ease my heart,
  But in their briny bed
My tears must stop, for every drop
  Hinders needle and thread!'

With fingers weary and worn,
  With eyelids heavy and red,
A woman sat, in unwomanly rags,
  Plying her needle and thread –
Stitch! stitch! stitch!
  In poverty, hunger, and dirt,
And still with a voice of dolorous pitch, –
Would that its tone could reach the Rich! –
  She sang this 'Song of the Shirt!'

The Bridge of Sighs

One more Unfortunate,
  Weary of breath,
Rashly importunate,
  Gone to her death!

Take her up tenderly,
  Lift her with care;
Fashion'd so slenderly
  Young, and so fair!

Look at her garments
Clinging like cerements;
Whilst the wave constantly
  Drips from her clothing;
Take her up instantly,
  Loving, not loathing.

Touch her not scornfully;
Think of her mournfully,
    Gently and humanly;
Not of the stains of her,
All that remains of her
    Now is pure womanly.

Make no deep scrutiny
Into her mutiny
    Rash and undutiful:
Past all dishonour,
Death has left on her
    Only the beautiful.

Still, for all slips of hers,
    One of Eve's family –
Wipe those poor lips of hers
    Oozing so clammily.

Loop up her tresses
    Escaped from the comb,
Her fair auburn tresses;
Whilst wonderment guesses
    Where was her home?

Who was her father?
    Who was her mother?
Had she a sister?
    Had she a brother?
Or was there a dearer one
Still, and a nearer one
    Yet, than all other?

Alas! for the rarity
Of Christian charity
    Under the sun!
O, it was pitiful!
Near a whole city full,
    Home she had none.

Sisterly, brotherly,
Fatherly, motherly
    Feelings had changed:
Love, by harsh evidence,
Thrown from its eminence;
Even God's providence
    Seeming estranged.

Where the lamps quiver
So far in the river,
    With many a light
From window and casement,
From garret to basement,
She stood, with amazement,
    Houseless by night.

The bleak wind of March
    Made her tremble and shiver;
But not the dark arch,
Or the black flowing river:
Mad from life's history,
Glad to death's mystery,
    Swift to be hurl'd –
Anywhere, anywhere
    Out of the world!

In she plunged boldly –
No matter how coldly
    The rough river ran –
Over the brink of it,
Picture it – think of it,
    Dissolute Man!
Lave in it, drink of it,
    Then, if you can!

Take her up tenderly,
    Lift her with care;
Fashion'd so slenderly,
    Young, and so fair!

Ere her limbs frigidly
Stiffen too rigidly,
    Decently, kindly,
Smooth and compose them;
And her eyes, close them,
    Staring so blindly!

Dreadfully staring
    Thro' muddy impurity,
As when with the daring
Last look of despairing
    Fix'd on futurity.

Perishing gloomily,
Spurr'd by contumely,
Cold inhumanity,
Burning insanity,
    Into her rest. –
Cross her hands humbly
As if praying dumbly,
    Over her breast!

Owning her weakness,
    Her evil behaviour,
And leaving, with meekness,
    Her sins to her Saviour!

I Remember, I Remember

I remember, I remember,
The house where I was born,
The little window where the sun
Came peeping in at morn;
He never came a wink too soon,
Nor brought too long a day,
But now, I often wish the night
Had borne my breath away!

I remember, I remember,
The roses, red and white,
The violets, and the lily-cups,
Those flowers made of light!
The lilacs where the robin built,
And where my brother set
The laburnum on his birthday, –
The tree is living yet!

I remember, I remember,
Where I was used to swing,
And thought the air must rush as fresh
To swallows on the wing;
My spirit flew in feathers then,
That is so heavy now,
And summer pools could hardly cool
The fever on my brow!

I remember, I remember,
The fir trees dark and high;
I used to think their slender tops
Were close against the sky:
It was a childish ignorance,
But now 'tis little joy
To know I'm farther off from heaven
Than when I was a boy.

LORD MACAULAY

Horatius

Lars Porsena of Clusium
  By the Nine Gods he swore
That the great house of Tarquin
  Should suffer wrong no more.
By the Nine Gods he swore it,
  And named a trysting day,
And bade his messangers ride forth,
East and west and south and north,
  To summon his array.

East and west and south and north
  The messengers ride fast,
And tower and town and cottage
  Have heard the trumpet's blast.
Shame on the false Etruscan
  Who lingers in his home,
When Porsena of Clusium
  Is on the march for Rome.

The horsemen and the footmen
  Are pouring in amain
From many a stately market-place;
  From many a fruitful plain;
From many a lonely hamlet,
  Which, hid by beech and pine,
Like an eagle's nest, hangs on the crest
  Of purple Apennine;

From lordly Volaterræ,
  Where scowls the far-famed hold
Piled by the hands of giants
  For godlike kings of old;
From seagirt Populonia,
  Whose sentinels descry
Sardinia's snowy mountain-tops
  Fringing the southern sky;

From the proud mart of Pisæ,
  Queen of the western waves,
Where ride Massilia's triremes
  Heavy with fair-haired slaves;
From where sweet Clanis wanders
  Through corn and vines and flowers;
From where Cortona lifts to heaven
  Her diadem of towers.

Tall are the oaks whose acorns
  Drop in dark Auser's rill;
Fat are the stags that champ the boughs
  Of the Ciminian hill;

Beyond all streams Clitumnus
  Is to the herdsman dear;
Best of all pools the fowler loves
  The great Volsinian mere.

But now no stroke of woodman
  Is heard by Auser's rill;
No hunter tracks the stag's green path
  Up the Ciminian hill;
Unwatched along Citumnus
  Grazes the milk-white steer;
Unharmed the water fowl may dip
  In the Volsinian mere.

The harvests of Arretium,
  This year, old men shall reap;
This year, young boys in Umbro
  Shall plunge the struggling sheep;
And in the vats of Luna,
  This year, the must shall foam
Round the white feet of laughing girls
  Whose sires have marched to Rome.

There be thirty chosen prophets,
  The wisest of the land,
Who alway by Lars Porsena
  Both morn and evening stand:
Evening and morn the Thirty
  Have turned the verses o'er,
Traced from the right on linen white
  By mighty seers of yore.

And with one voice the Thirty
  Have their glad answer given:
'Go forth, go forth, Lars Porsena;
  Go forth, beloved of Heaven;
Go, and return in glory
  To Clusium's royal dome;
And hang round Nurscia's altars
  The golden shields of Rome.'

And now hath every city
  Sent up her tale of men;
The foot are fourscore thousand,
  The horse are thousands ten.
Before the gates of Sutrium
  Is met the great array.
A proud man was Lars Porsena
  Upon the trysting day.

For all the Etruscan armies
  Were ranged beneath his eye,
And many a banished Roman,
  And many a stout ally;
And with a mighty following
  To join the muster came
The Tusculan Mamilius,
  Prince of the Latian name.

But by the yellow Tiber
  Was tumult and affright:
From all the spacious champaign
  To Rome men took their flight.
A mile around the city,
  The throng stopped up the ways:
A fearful sight it was to see
  Through two long nights and days

For aged folks on crutches,
  And women great with child,
And mothers sobbing over babes
  That clung to them and smiled.
And sick men borne in litters
  High on the necks of slaves,
And troops of sun-burned husbandmen
  With reaping-hooks and staves,

And droves of mules and asses
  Laden with skins of wine,
And endless flocks of goats and sheep,
  And endless herds of kine,

And endless trains of waggons
　　That creaked beneath the weight
Of corn-sacks and of household goods,
　　Choked every roaring gate.

Now, from the rock Tarpeian,
　　Could the wan burghers spy
The line of blazing villages
　　Red in the midnight sky.
The Fathers of the City,
　　They sat all night and day,
For every hour some horseman came
　　With tidings of dismay.

To eastward and to westward
　　Have spread the Tuscan bands;
Nor house, nor fence, nor dovecote
　　In Crustumerium stands.
Verbenna down to Ostia
　　Hath wasted all the plain;
Astur hath stormed Janiculum,
　　And the stout guards are slain.

I wis, in all the Senate,
　　There was no heart so bold,
But sore it ached, and fast it beat,
　　When that ill news was told.
Forthwith up rose the Consul,
　　Up rose the Fathers all;
In haste they girded up their gowns,
　　And hied them to the wall.

They held a council standing
　　Before the River-Gate;
Short time was there, ye well may guess,
　　For musing or debate.
Out spake the Consul roundly:
　　'The bridge must straight go down;
For, since Janiculum is lost,
　　Nought else can save the town.'

Just then a scout came flying,
    All wild with haste and fear:
'To arms! to arms! Sir Consul:
    Lars Porsena is here.'
On the low hills to westward
    The Consul fixed his eye,
And saw the swarthy storm of dust
    Rise fast along the sky.

And nearer fast and nearer
    Doth the red whirlwind come;
And louder still and still more loud,
From underneath that rolling cloud,
Is heard the trumpet's war-note proud
    The trampling, and the hum.
And plainly and more plainly
    Now through the gloom appears,
Far to left and far to right.
In broken gleams of dark-blue light,
The long array of helmets bright,
    The long array of spears.

And plainly and more plainly,
    Above that glimmering line,
Now might ye see the banners
    Of twelve fair cities shine;
But the banner of proud Clusium
    Was highest of them all,
The terror of the Umbrian,
    The terror of the Gaul.

And plainly and more plainly
    Now might the burghers know,
By port and vest, by horse and crest,
    Each warlike Lucumo.
There Cilnius of Arretium
    On his fleet roan was seen;
And Astur of the four-fold shield,
Girt with the brand none else may wield,
Tolumnius with the belt of gold,
And dark Verbenna from the hold
    By reedy Thrasymene.

Fast by the royal standard,
  O'erlooking all the war,
Lars Porsena of Clusium
  Sat in his ivory car.
By the right wheel rode Mamilius,
  Prince of the Latian name;
And by the left false Sextus,
  That wrought the deed of shame.

But when the face of Sextus
  Was seen among the foes,
A yell that rent the firmament
  From all the town arose.
On the house-tops was no woman
  But spat towards him and hissed
No child but screamed out curses,
  And shook its little fist.

But the Consul's brow was sad,
  And the Consul's speech was low,
And darkly looked he at the wall,
  And darkly at the foe.
'Their van will be upon us
  Before the bridge goes down;
And if they once may win the bridge,
  What hope to save the town?'

Then out spake brave Horatius,
  The Captain of the Gate:
'To every man upon this earth
  Death cometh soon or late.
And how can man die better
  Than facing fearful odds,
For the ashes of his fathers,
  And the temples of his Gods,

'And for the tender mother
  Who dandled him to rest,
And for the wife who nurses
  His baby at her breast,

And for the holy maidens
    Who feed the eternal flame,
To save them from false Sextus
    That wrought the deed of shame?

'Hew down the bridge, Sir Consul,
    With all the speed ye may;
I, with two more to help me,
    Will hold the foe in play.
In yon strait path a thousand
    May well be stopped by three.
Now who will stand on either hand,
    And keep the bridge with me?'

Then out spake Spurius Lartius;
    A Ramnian proud was he:
'Lo, I will stand at thy right hand,
    And keep the bridge with thee.'
And out spake strong Herminius;
    Of Titian blood was he:
'I will abide on thy left side,
    And keep the bridge with thee.'

'Horatius,' quoth the Consul,
    'As thou sayest, so let it be.'
And straight against that great array
    Forth went the dauntless Three.
For Romans in Rome's quarrel
    Spared neither land nor gold,
Nor son nor wife, nor limb nor life,
    In the brave days of old.

Then none was for a party;
    Then all were for the state;
Then the great man helped the poor,
    And the poor man loved the great.
Then lands were fairly portioned;
    Then spoils were fairly sold:
The Romans were like brothers
    In the brave days of old.

Now Roman is to Roman
  More hateful than a foe,
And the Tribunes beard the high,
  And the Fathers grind the low.
As we wax hot in faction,
  In battle we wax cold:
Wherefore men fight not as they fought
  In the brave days of old.

Now while the Three were tightening
  Their harness on their backs,
The Consul was the foremost man
  To take in hand an axe:
And Fathers mixed with Commons
  Seized hatchet, bar, and crow,
And smote upon the planks above,
  And loosed the props below.

Meanwhile the Tuscan army,
  Right glorious to behold,
Came flashing back the noonday light,
Rank behind rank, like surges bright
  Of a broad sea of gold.
Four hundred trumpets sounded
  A peal of warlike glee,
As that great host, with measured tread,
And spears advanced, and ensigns spread,
Rolled slowly towards the bridge's head,
  Where stood the dauntless Three.

The Three stood calm and silent,
  And looked upon the foes,
And a great shout of laughter
  From all the vanguard rose:
And forth three chiefs came spurring
  Before that deep array;
To earth they sprang, their swords they drew,
And lifted high their shields, and flew
  To win the narrow way;

Aunus from green Tifernum,
    Lord of the Hill of Vines;
And Seius, whose eight hundred slaves
    Sicken in Ilva's mines;
And Picus, long to Clusium
    Vassal in peace and war,
Who led to fight his Umbrian powers
From that grey crag where, girt with towers,
The fortress of Nequinum lowers
    O'er the pale waves of Nar.

Stout Lartius hurled down Aunus
    Into the stream beneath:
Herminius struck at Seius,
    And clove him to the teeth:
At Picus brave Horatius
    Darted one fiery thrust;
And the proud Umbrian's gilded arms
    Clashed in the bloody dust.

Then Ocnus of Falerii
    Rushed on the Roman Three;
And Lausulus of Urgo,
    The rover of the sea;
And Aruns of Volsinium,
    Who slew the great wild boar,
The great wild boar that had his den
Amidst the reeds of Cosa's fen,
And wasted fields, and slaughtered men,
    Along Albinia's shore.

Herminius smote down Aruns:
    Lartius laid Ocnus low:
Right to the heart of Lausulus
    Horatius sent a blow.
'Lie there,' he cried, 'fell pirate!
    No more, aghast and pale,
From Ostia's walls the crowd shall mark
The track of thy destroying bark.
No more Campania's hinds shall fly
To woods and caverns when they spy
    Thy thrice accursed sail.'

But now no sound of laughter
    Was heard among the foes.
A wild and wrathful clamour
    From all the vanguard rose.
Six spears' lengths from the entrance
    Halted that deep array,
And for a space no man came forth
    To win the narrow way.

But hark! the cry is Astur:
    And lo! the ranks divide;
And the great Lord of Luna
    Comes with his stately stride.
Upon his ample shoulders
    Clangs loud the four-fold shield,
And in his hand he shakes the brand
    Which none but he can wield.

He smiled on those bold Romans
    A smile serene and high;
He eyed the flinching Tuscans,
    And scorn was in his eye.
Quoth he, 'The she-wolf's litter
    Stand savagely at bay:
But will ye dare to follow,
    If Astur clears the way?'

Then, whirling up his broadsword
    With both hands to the height,
He rushed against Horatius,
    And smote with all his might.
With shield and blade Horatius
    Right deftly turned the blow.
The blow, though turned, came yet too nigh;
It missed his helm, but gashed his thigh:
The Tuscans raised a joyful cry
    To see the red blood flow.

He reeled, and on Herminius
    He leaned one breathing-space;

Then, like a wild cat mad with wounds,
  Sprang right at Astur's face.
Through teeth, and skull, and helmet
  So fierce a thrust he sped,
The good sword stood a hand-breadth out
  Behind the Tuscan's head.

And the great Lord of Luna
  Fell at that deadly stroke,
As falls on Mount Alvernus
  A thunder-smitten oak.
Far o'er the crashing forest
  The giant arms lie spread;
And the pale augurs, muttering low,
  Gaze on the blasted head.

On Astur's throat Horatius
  Right firmly pressed his heel,
And thrice and four times tugged amain,
  Ere he wrenched out the steel.
'And see,' he cried, 'the welcome,
  Fair guests, that waits you here!
What noble Lucumo comes next
  To taste our Roman cheer?'

But at his haughty challenge
  A sullen murmur ran,
Mingled of wrath, and shame, and dread,
  Along that glittering van.
There lacked not men of prowess,
  Nor men of lordly race;
For all Etruria's noblest
  Were round the fatal place.

But all Etruria's noblest
  Felt their hearts sink to see
On the earth the bloody corpses,
  In the path the dauntless Three;
And, from the ghastly entrance
  Where those bold Romans stood,
All shrank, like boys who unaware,

Ranging the woods to start a hare,
Come to the mouth of a dark lair
Where, growling low, a fierce old bear
  Lies amidst bones and blood.

Was none who would be foremost
  To lead such dire attack:
But those behind cried 'Forward!'
  And those before cried 'Back!'
And backward now and forward
  Wavers the deep array;
And on the tossing sea of steel,
To and fro the standards reel;
And the victorious trumpet-peal
  Dies fitfully away.

Yet one man for one moment
  Strode out before the crowd;
Well known was he to all the Three,
  And they gave him greeting loud.
'Now welcome, welcome, Sextus!
  Now welcome to thy home!
Why dost thou stay, and turn away?
  Here lies the road to Rome.'

Thrice looked he at the city;
  Thrice looked he at the dead;
And thrice came on in fury,
  And thrice turned back in dread:
And, white with fear and hatred,
  Scowled at the narrow way
Where, wallowing in a pool of blood,
  The bravest Tuscans lay.

But meanwhile axe and lever
  Have manfully been plied;
And now the bridge hangs tottering
  Above the boiling tide.
'Come back, come back, Horatius!'
  Loud cried the Fathers all.
'Back, Lartius! back, Herminius!
  Back, ere the ruin fall!'

Back darted Spurius Lartius;
  Herminius darted back:
And, as they passed, beneath their feet
  They felt the timbers crack.
But when they turned their faces,
  And on the farther shore
Saw brave Horatius stand alone,
  They would have crossed once more.

But with a crash like thunder
  Fell every loosened beam,
And, like a dam, the mighty wreck
  Lay right athwart the stream:
And a long shout of triumph
  Rose from the walls of Rome,
As to the highest turret-tops
  Was splashed the yellow foam.

And, like a horse unbroken
  When first he feels the rein,
The furious river struggled hard,
  And tossed his tawny mane,
And burst the curb, and bounded,
  Rejoicing to be free,
And whirling down, in fierce career,
Battlement, and plank, and pier,
  Rushed headlong to the sea.

Alone stood brave Horatius,
  But constant still in mind;
Thrice thirty thousand foes before,
  And the broad flood behind.
'Down with him!' cried false Sextus,
  With a smile on his pale face.
'Now yield thee,' cried Lars Porsena,
  'Now yield thee to our grace.'

Round turned he, as not deigning
  Those craven ranks to see;
Nought spake he to Lars Porsena,
  To Sextus nought spake he;

But he saw on Palatinus
  The white porch of his home;
And he spake to the noble river
  That rolls by the towers of Rome.

'Oh, Tiber! father Tiber!
  To whom the Romans pray,
A Roman's life, a Roman's arms,
  Take thou in charge this day!'
So he spake, and speaking sheathed
  The good sword by his side,
And with his harness on his back,
  Plunged headlong in the tide.

No sound of joy or sorrow
  Was heard from either bank;
But friends and foes in dumb surprise,
With parted lips and straining eyes,
  Stood gazing where he sank;
And when above the surges
  They saw his crest appear,
All Rome sent forth a rapturous cry,
And even the ranks of Tuscany
  Could scarce forbear to cheer.

But fiercely ran the current,
  Swollen high by months of rain:
And fast his blood was flowing;
  And he was sore in pain,
And heavy with his armour,
  And spent with changing blows:
And oft they thought him sinking,
  But still again he rose.

Never, I ween, did swimmer,
  In such an evil case,
Struggle through such a raging flood
  Safe to the landing place:
But his limbs were borne up bravely
  By the brave heart within,
And our good father Tiber
  Bare bravely up his chin.

'Curse on him!' quoth false Sextus;
  'Will not the villain drown?
But for this stay, ere close of day
  We should have sacked the town!'
'Heaven help him!' quoth Lars Porsena,
  'And bring him safe to shore;
For such a gallant feat of arms
  Was never seen before.'

And now he feels the bottom:
  Now on dry earth he stands;
Now round him throng the Fathers
  To press his gory hands;
And now, with shouts and clapping,
  And noise of weeping loud,
He enters through the River-Gate,
  Borne by the joyous crowd.

They gave him of the corn-land,
  That was of public right,
As much as two strong oxen
  Could plough from morn till night;
And they made a molten image,
  And set it up on high,
And there it stands unto this day
  To witness if I lie.

It stands in the Comitium,
  Plain for all folk to see;
Horatius in his harness,
  Halting upon one knee:
And underneath is written,
  In letters all of gold,
How valiantly he kept the bridge
  In the brave days of old.

And still his name sounds stirring
  Unto the men of Rome,
As the trumpet-blast that cries to them
  To charge the Volscian home;
And wives still pray to Juno
  For boys with hearts as bold

As his who kept the bridge so well
  In the brave days of old.

And in the nights of winter,
  When the cold north winds blow,
And the long howling of the wolves
  Is heard amidst the snow;
When round the lonely cottage
  Roars loud the tempest's din,
And the good logs of Algidus
  Roar louder yet within;

When the oldest cask is opened,
  And the largest lamp is lit;
When the chestnuts glow in the embers,
  And the kid turns on the spit;
When young and old in circle
  Around the firebrands close;
When the girls are weaving baskets,
  And the lads are shaping bows

When the goodman mends his armour,
  And trims his helmet's plume;
When the goodwife's shuttle merrily
  Goes flashing through the loom;
With weeping and with laughter
  Still is the story told,
How well Horatius kept the bridge
  In the brave days of old.

The Armada

Attend, all ye who list to hear our noble England's praise;
I tell of the thrice famous deeds she wrought in ancient days,
When that great fleet invincible against her bore in vain
The richest spoils of Mexico, the stoutest hearts of Spain.

It was about the lovely close of a warm summer day,
There came a gallant merchant-ship full sail to Plymouth Bay;

Her crew hath seen Castile's black fleet, beyond Aurigny's isle,
At earliest twilight, on the waves lie heaving many a mile.
At sunrise she escaped their van, by God's especial grace;
And the tall Pinta, till the noon, had held her close in chase.
Forthwith a guard at every gun was placed along the wall;
The beacon blazed upon the roof of Edgecumbe's lofty hall;
Many a light fishing-bark put out to pry along the coast,
And with loose rein and bloody spur rode inland many a post.
With his white hair unbonneted, the stout old sheriff comes;
Behind him march the halberdiers; before him sound the
    drums;
His yeomen round the market cross make clear an ample space;
For there behoves him to set up the standard of Her Grace.
And haughtily the trumpets peal, and gaily dance the bells,
As slow upon the labouring wind the royal blazon swells.
Look how the Lion of the sea lifts up his ancient crown,
And underneath his deadly paw treads the gay lilies down.
So stalked he when he turned to flight, on that famed Picard
    field,
Bohemia's plume, and Genoa's bow, and Cæsar's eagle shield.
So glared he when at Agincourt in wrath he turned to bay,
And crushed and torn beneath his claws the princely hunters
    lay.
Ho! strike the flagstaff deep, sir Knight: ho! scatter flowers,
    fair maids:
Ho! gunners, fire a loud salute: ho! gallants, draw your blades:
Thou sun, shine on her joyously; ye breezes, waft her wide;
Our glorious SEMPER EADEM, the banner of our pride.
    The freshening breeze of eve unfurled that banner's massy
        fold;
The parting gleam of sunshine kissed that haughty scroll of
        gold;
Night sank upon the dusky beach, and on the purple sea,
Such night in England ne'er had been, nor e'er again shall be.
From Eddystone to Berwick bounds, from Lynn to Milford
        Bay,
That time of slumber was as bright and busy as the day;
For swift to east and swift to west the ghastly war-flame spread,
High on St. Michael's Mount it shone: it shone on Beachy
        Head.
Far on the deep the Spaniard saw, along each southern shire,

Cape beyond cape, in endless range, those twinkling points of
fire.
The fisher left his skiff to rock on Tamar's glittering waves:
The rugged miners poured to war from Mendip's sunless
caves:
O'er Longleat's towers, o'er Cranbourne's oaks, the fiery
herald flew:
He roused the shepherds of Stonehenge, the rangers of Beaulieu.
Right sharp and quick the bells all night rang out from Bristol
town,
And ere the day three hundred horse had met on Clifton
down;
The sentinel on Whitehall gate looked forth into the night,
And saw o'erhanging Richmond Hill the streak of blood-red
light.
Then bugle's note and cannon's roar the deathlike silence broke,
And with one start, and with one cry, the royal city woke.
At once on all her stately gates arose the answering fires;
At once the wild alarum clashed from all her reeling spires;
From all the batteries of the Tower pealed loud the voice of
fear;
And all the thousand masts of Thames sent back a louder cheer:
And from the furthest wards was heard the rush of hurrying
feet,
And the broad streams of pikes and flags rushed down each
roaring street;
And broader still became the blaze, and louder still the din,
As fast from every village round the horse came spurring in:
And eastward straight from wild Blackheath the warlike
errand went,
And roused in many an ancient hall the gallant squires of Kent.
Southward from Surrey's pleasant hills flew those bright
couriers forth;
High on bleak Hampstead's swarthy moor they started for the
north;
And on, and on, without a pause, untired they bounded still:
All night from tower to tower they sprang; they sprang from
hill to hill:
Till the proud peak unfurled the flag o'er Darwin's rocky
dales,
Till like volcanoes flared to heaven the stormy hills of Wales,

Till twelve fair counties saw the blaze on Malvern's lonely
   height,
Till streamed in crimson on the wind the Wrekin's crest of
   light,
Till broad and fierce the star came forth on Ely's stately fane,
And tower and hamlet rose in arms o'er all the boundless
   plain;
Till Belvoir's lordly terraces the sign to Lincoln sent,
And Lincoln sped the message on o'er the wide vale of Trent;
Till Skiddaw saw the fire that burned on Gaunt's embattled
   pile,
And the red glare on Skiddaw roused the burghers of Carlisle.

A Jacobite's Epitaph

To my true king I offered free from stain
Courage and faith; vain faith, and courage vain.
For him I threw lands, honours, wealth, away,
And one dear hope, that was more prized than they.
For him I languished in a foreign clime,
Gray-haired with sorrow in my manhood's prime;
Heard on Lavernia Scargill's whispering trees,
And pined by Arno for my lovelier Tees;
Beheld each night my home in fevered sleep,
Each morning started from the dream to weep;
Till God, who saw me tried too sorely, gave
The resting-place I asked, an early grave.
O thou, whom chance leads to this nameless stone,
From that proud country which was once mine own,
By those white cliffs I never more must see,
By that dear language which I spake like thee,
Forget all feuds, and shed one English tear
O'er English dust. A broken heart lies here.

CARDINAL NEWMAN

Lead, Kindly Light

Lead, kindly Light, amid the encircling gloom,
        Lead thou me on;
The night is dark, and I am far from home,
        Lead thou me on.
Keep thou my feet; I do not ask to see
The distant scene; one step enough for me.

I was not ever thus, nor prayed that thou
        Should'st lead me on;
I loved to choose and see my path; but now
        Lead thou me on.
I loved the garish day, and, spite of fears,
Pride ruled my will: remember not past years.

So long thy power hath blest me, sure it still
        Will lead me on
O'er moor and fen, o'er crag and torrent, till
        The night is gone,
And with the morn those angel faces smile,
Which I have loved long since, and lost awhile.

ROBERT S. HAWKER

The Song of the Western Men

A good sword and a trusty hand!
    A merry heart and true!
King James's men shall understand
    What Cornish lads can do.

And have they fixed the where and when?
    And shall Trelawny die?
Here's twenty thousand Cornish men
    Will know the reason why!

Out spake their captain brave and bold,
   A merry wight was he:
'If London Tower were Michael's hold,
   We'd set Trelawny free!

'We'll cross the Tamar, land to land,
   The Severn is no stay,
With "one and all," and hand in hand,
   And who shall bid us nay?

'And when we come to London Wall,
   A pleasant sight to view,
Come forth! come forth! ye cowards all,
   Here's men as good as you.

'Trelawny he's in keep and hold,
   Trelawny he may die;
But here's twenty thousand Cornish bold
   Will know the reason why!'

RALPH WALDO EMERSON

Concord Hymn

commemorating the American Revolution

By the rude bridge that arched the flood,
   Their flag to April's breeze unfurled,
Here once the embattled farmers stood,
   And fired the shot heard round the world.

The foe long since in silence slept;
   Alike the conqueror silent sleeps;
And Time the ruined bridge has swept
   Down the dark stream which seaward creeps.

On this green bank, by this soft stream,
   We set to-day a votive stone;
That memory may their deed redeem,
   When, like our sires, our sons are gone.

Spirit, that made those heroes dare
　　To die, or leave their children free,
Bid Time and Nature gently spare
　　The shaft we raise to them and thee.

HENRY WADSWORTH LONGFELLOW

The Wreck of the Hesperus

It was the schooner Hesperus,
　　That sailed the wintry sea;
And the skipper had taken his little daughter,
　　To bear him company.

Blue were her eyes as the fairy-flax,
　　Her cheeks like the dawn of day,
And her bosom white as the hawthorn buds
　　That ope in the month of May.

The skipper he stood beside the helm,
　　His pipe was in his mouth,
And he watched how the veering flaw did blow
　　The smoke now West, now South.

Then up and spake an old Sailor,
　　Had sailed the Spanish Main,
'I pray thee, put into yonder port,
　　For I fear a hurricane.

'Last night the moon had a golden ring,
　　And to-night no moon we see!'
The skipper he blew a whiff from his pipe,
　　And a scornful laugh laughed he.

Colder and colder blew the wind,
　　A gale from the North-east;
The snow fell hissing in the brine,
　　And the billows frothed like yeast.

Down came the storm, and smote amain,
    The vessel in its strength;
She shuddered and paused, like a frightened steed,
    Then leaped her cable's length.

'Come hither! come hither! my little daughtèr,
    And do not tremble so;
For I can weather the roughest gale,
    That ever wind did blow.'

He wrapped her warm in his seaman's coat
    Against the stinging blast;
He cut a rope from a broken spar,
    And bound her to the mast.

'O father! I hear the churchbells ring,
    O say, what may it be?'
''Tis a fog-bell on a rock-bound coast!' –
    And he steered for the open sea.

'O father! I hear the sound of guns,
    O say, what may it be?'
'Some ship in distress, that cannot live
    In such an angry sea!'

'O father! I see a gleaming light,
    O say, what may it be?'
But the father answered never a word,
    A frozen corpse was he.

Lashed to the helm, all stiff and stark,
    With his face turned to the skies,
The lantern gleamed through the gleaming snow
    On his fixed and glassy eyes.

Then the maiden clasped her hands and prayed
    That savèd she might be;
And she thought of Christ, who stilled the wave,
    On the Lake of Galilee.

And fast through the midnight dark and drear,
    Through the whistling sleet and snow,
Like a sheeted ghost, the vessel swept
    Towards the reef of Norman's Woe.

And ever the fitful gusts between
    A sound came from the land;
It was the sound of the trampling surf,
    On the rocks and the hard sea-sand.

The breakers were right beneath her bows,
    She drifted a dreary wreck,
And a whooping billow swept the crew
    Like icicles from her deck.

She struck where the white and fleecy waves
    Looked soft as carded wool,
But the cruel rocks, they gored her side
    Like the horns of an angry bull.

Her rattling shrouds, all sheathed in ice,
    With the masts went by the board;
Like a vessel of glass, she stove and sank,
    Ho! ho! the breakers roared!

At daybreak, on the bleak sea-beach,
    A fisherman stood aghast,
To see the form of a maiden fair,
    Lashed close to a drifting mast.

The salt sea was frozen on her breast,
    The salt tears in her eyes;
And he saw her hair, like the brown sea-weed,
    On the billows fall and rise.

Such was the wreck of the Hesperus,
    In the midnight and the snow!
Christ save us all from a death like this
    On the reef of Norman's Woe!

The Village Blacksmith

Under a spreading chestnut tree
  The village smithy stands;
The smith, a mighty man is he,
  With large and sinewy hands;
And the muscles of his brawny arms
  Are strong as iron bands.

His hair is crisp, and black, and long,
  His face is like the tan;
His brow is wet with honest sweat,
  He earns whate'er he can,
And looks the whole world in the face,
  For he owes not any man.

Week in, week out, from morn till night,
  You can hear his bellows blow;
You can hear him swing his heavy sledge,
  With measured beat and slow,
Like a sexton ringing the village bell,
  When the evening sun is low.

And children coming home from school
  Look in at the open door;
They love to see the flaming forge,
  And hear the bellows roar,
And catch the burning sparks that fly
  Like chaff from a threshing floor.

He goes on Sunday to the church,
  And sits among his boys;
He hears the parson pray and preach,
  He hears his daughter's voice,
Singing in the village choir,
  And it makes his heart rejoice.

It sounds to him like her mother's voice,
  Singing in Paradise!
He needs must think of her once more,
  How in the grave she lies;

And with his hard, rough hand he wipes
  A tear out of his eyes.

Toiling, – rejoicing, – sorrowing,
  Onward through life he goes;
Each morning sees some task begin,
  Each evening sees it close;
Something attempted, something done,
  Has earned a night's repose.

Thanks, thanks to thee, my worthy friend,
  For the lesson thou hast taught!
Thus at the flaming forge of life
  Our fortunes must be wrought;
Thus on its sounding anvil shaped
  Each burning deed and thought!

Excelsior

The shades of night were falling fast,
As through an Alpine village passed
A youth, who bore, 'mid snow and ice,
A banner with the strange device,
    Excelsior!

His brow was sad; his eye beneath
Flashed like a falchion from its sheath,
And like a silver clarion rung
The accents of that unknown tongue,
    Excelsior!

In happy homes he saw the light
Of household fires gleam warm and bright;
Above, the spectral glaciers shone,
And from his lips escaped a groan,
    Excelsior!

'Try not the Pass!' the old man said;
'Dark lowers the tempest overhead,

The roaring torrent is deep and wide!
And loud that clarion voice replied,
      Excelsior!

'O stay,' the maiden said, 'and rest
Thy weary head upon this breast!'
A tear stood in his bright blue eye,
But still he answered, with a sigh,
      Excelsior!

'Beware the pine-tree's withered branch!
Beware the awful avalanche!'
This was the peasant's last Goodnight,
A voice replied, far up the height,
      Excelsior!

At break of day, as heavenward
The pious monks of Saint Bernard
Uttered the oft-repeated prayer,
A voice cried through the startled air,
      Excelsior!

A traveller, by the faithful hound,
Half-buried in the snow was found,
Still grasping in his hand of ice
That banner with the strange device,
      Excelsior!

There in the twilight cold and gray,
Lifeless, but beautiful, he lay,
And from the sky, serene and far,
A voice fell, like a falling star,
      Excelsior!

My Lost Youth

    Often I think of the beautiful town
      That is seated by the sea;
    Often in thought go up and down

The pleasant streets of that dear old town.
   And my youth comes back to me,
    And a verse of a Lapland song
    Is haunting my memory still:
  'A boy's will is the wind's will,
And the thoughs of youth are long, long thoughts.'

I can see the shadowy lines of its trees,
   And catch, in sudden gleams,
The sheen of the far-surrounding seas,
And islands that were the Hesperides
    Of all my boyish dreams.
    And the burden of that old song,
    It murmurs and whispers still:
  'A boy's will is the wind's will,
And the thoughts of youth are long, long thoughts.'

I remember the black wharves and the slips,
   And the sea-tides tossing free;
And Spanish sailors with bearded lips,
And the beauty and mystery of the ships,
    And the magic of the sea.
    And the voice of that wayward song,
    Is singing and saying still:
  'A boy's will is the wind's will,
And the thoughts of youth are long, long thoughts.'

I remember the bulwarks by the shore,
   And the fort upon the hill;
The sunrise gun, with its hollow roar,
The drum-beat repeated o'er and o'er,
    And the bugle wild and shrill.
    And the music of that old song
    Throbs in my memory still:
  'A boy's will is the wind's will,
And the thoughts of youth are long, long thoughts.'

I remember the sea-fight far away,
   How it thundered o'er the tide!
And the dead captains, as they lay

In their graves, o'erlooking the tranquil bay,
   Where they in battle died.
     And the sound of that mournful song
     Goes through me with a thrill:
   'A boy's will is the wind's will,
And the thoughts of youth are long, long thoughts.'

I can see the breezy dome of groves,
   The shadows of Deering's Woods;
And the friendships old and the early loves
Come back with a Sabbath sound, as of doves
   In quiet neighbourhoods.
     And the verse of that sweet old song,
     It flutters and murmurs still:
   'A boy's will is the wind's will,
And the thoughts of youth are long, long thoughts.'

I remember the gleams and glooms that dart
   Across the schoolboy's brain;
The song and the silence in the heart,
That in part are prophecies, and in part
   Are longings wild and vain.
     And the voice of that fitful song
     Sings on, and is never still:
   'A boy's will is the wind's will,
And the thoughts of youth are long, long thoughts.'

There are things of which I may not speak;
   There are dreams that cannot die;
There are thoughts that make the strong heart weak,
And bring a pallor into the cheek,
   And a mist before the eye.
     And the words to that fatal song
     Come over me like a chill:
   'A boy's will is the wind's will,
And the thoughts of youth are long, long thoughts.'

Strange to me now are the forms I meet
   When I visit the dear old town;
But the native air is pure and sweet,

And the trees that o'ershadow each well-known street,
　　As they balance up and down,
　　　　Are singing the beautiful song,
　　　　Are sighing and whispering still:
　　'A boy's will is the wind's will,
And the thoughts of youth are long, long thoughts.'

And Deering's Woods are fresh and fair,
　　And with joy that is almost pain
My heart goes back to wander there,
And among the dreams of the days that were,
　　I find my lost youth again.
　　　　And the strange and beautiful song,
　　　　The groves are repeating it still:
　　'A boy's will is the wind's will,
And the thoughts of youth are long, long thoughts.'

Paul Revere's Ride

Listen, my children, and you shall hear
Of the midnight ride of Paul Revere,
On the eighteenth of April, in Seventy-five;
Hardly a man is now alive
Who remembers that famous day and year.
He said to his friend, 'If the British march
By land or sea from the town tonight,
Hang a lantern aloft in the belfry arch
Of the North Church tower as a signal light, –
One, if by land, and two, if by sea;
And I on the opposite shore will be,
Ready to ride and spread the alarm
Through every Middlesex village and farm,
For the country-folk to be up and arm.'

Thee he said, 'Good night!' and with muffled oar
Silently rowed to the Charlestown shore,
Just as the moon rose over the bay,
Where swinging wide at her moorings lay
The Somerset, British man-of-war;

136

A phantom ship, with each mast and spar
Across the moon like a prison bar,
And a huge black hulk, that was magnified
By its own reflection in the tide.

Meanwhile, his friend, through alley and street,
Wanders and watches with eager ears,
Till in silence around him he hears
The muster of men at the barrack door,
The sound of arms, and the tramp of feet,
And the measured tread of the grenadiers,
Marching down to their boats on the shore.

Then he climbed to the tower of the church,
Up the wooden stairs, with stealthy tread,
To the belfry-chamber overhead,
And startled the pigeons from their perch
On the sombre rafters, that round him made
Masses and moving shapes of shade –
Up the trembling ladder, steep and tall,
To the highest window in the wall,
Where he paused to listen and look down
A moment on the roofs of the town,
And the moonlight flowing over all.

Beneath, in the churchyard, lay the dead,
In their night-encampment on the hill,
Wrapped in silence so deep and still
That he could hear, like a sentinel's tread,
The watchful night-wind, as it went
Creeping along from tent to tent,
And seeming to whisper, 'All is well!'

A moment only he feels the spell
Of the place and the hour, and the secret dread
Of the lonely belfry and the dead;
For suddenly all his thoughts are bent
On a shadowy something far away,
Where the river widens to meet the bay, –
A line of black that bends and floats
On the rising tide, like a bridge of boats.

Meanwhile, impatient to mount and ride,
Booted and spurred, with a heavy stride
On the opposite shore walked Paul Revere.
Now he patted his horse's side,
Now gazed at the landscape far and near,
Then, impetuous, stamped the earth,
And turned and tightened his saddle-girth;
But mostly he watched with eager search
The belfry-tower of the Old North Church.

As it rose above the graves on the hill,
Lonely and spectral and sombre and still.
And lo! as he looks, on the belfry's height
A glimmer, and then a gleam of light!
He springs to the saddle, the bridle he turns,
But lingers and gazes, till full on his sight
A second lamp in the belfry burns!

A hurry of hoofs in a village street,
A shape in the moonlight, a bulk in the dark,
And beneath, from the pebbles, in passing, a spark
Struck out by a steed flying fearless and fleet;
That was all! And yet, through the gloom and the light,
The fate of a nation was riding that night;
And the spark struck out by that steed, in his flight,
Kindled the land into flame with its heat.

He has left the village and mounted the steep,
And beneath him, tranquil and broad and deep,
Is the Mystic, meeting the ocean tides;
And under the alders, that skirt its edge,
Now soft on the sand, now loud on the ledge,
Is heard the tramp of his steed as he rides.

It was twelve by the village clock
When he crossed the bridge into Medford town.
He heard the crowing of the cock,
And the barking of the farmer's dog,
And felt the damp of the river fog,
That rises after the sun goes down.

It was one by the village clock,
When he galloped into Lexington.
He saw the gilded weathercock
Swim in the moonlight as he passed,
And the meeting-house windows, blank and bare,
Gaze at him with a spectral glare,
As if they already stood aghast
At the bloody work they would look upon.

It was two by the village clock,
When he came to the bridge in Concord town.
He heard the bleating of the flock,
And the twitter of birds among the trees,
And felt the breath of the morning breeze
Blowing over the meadows brown.
And one was safe and asleep in his bed
Who at the bridge would be first to fall,
Who that day would be lying dead,
Pierced by a British musket-ball.

You know the rest. In the books you have read,
How the British Regulars fired and fled, –
How the farmers gave them ball for ball,
From behind each fence and farmyard wall,
Chasing the red-coats down the lane,
Then crossing the fields to emerge again
Under the trees at the turn of the road,
And only pausing to fire and load.

So through the night rode Paul Revere;
And so through the night went his cry of alarm
To every Middlesex village and farm, –
A cry of defiance and not of fear,
A voice in the darkness, a knock at the door,
And a word that shall echo for evermore!
For, borne on the night-wind of the Past,
Through all our history, to the last,
In the hour of darkness and peril and need.
The people will waken and listen to hear
The hurrying hoof-beats of that steed,
And the midnight message of Paul Revere.

The Slave's Dream

Beside the ungathered rice he lay,
  His sickle in his hand;
His breast was bare, his matted hair
  Was buried in the sand.
Again, in the mist and shadow of sleep,
  He saw his Native Land.

Wide through the landscape of his dreams
  The lordly Niger flowed;
Beneath the palm-trees on the plain
  Once more a king he strode;
And heard the tinkling caravans
  Descend the mountain-road.

He saw once more his dark-eyed queen
  Among her children stand;
They clasped his neck, they kissed his cheeks,
  They held him by the hand! –
A tear burst from the sleeper's lids
  And fell into the sand.

And then at furious speed he rode
  Along the Niger's bank;
His bridle-reins were golden chains,
  And, with a martial clank,
At each leap he could feel his scabbard of steel
  Smiting his stallion's flank.

Before him, like a blood-red flag,
  The bright flamingoes flew;
From morn till night he followed their flight,
  O'er plains where the tamarind grew,
Till he saw the roofs of Caffre huts,
  And the ocean rose to view.

At night he heard the lion roar,
  And the hyena scream,
And the river-horse, as he crushed the reeds
  Beside some hidden stream;

And it passed, like a glorious roll of drums,
    Through the triumph of his dream.

The forests, with their myriad tongues,
    Shouted of liberty;
And the Blast of the Desert cried aloud,
    With a voice so wild and free,
That he started in his sleep and smiled
    At their tempestuous glee.

He did not feel the driver's whip,
    Nor the burning heat of day;
For Death had illumined the Land of Sleep,
    And his lifeless body lay
A worn-out fetter, that the soul
    Had broken and thrown away!

JOHN GREENLEAF WHITTIER

Barbara Frietchie

Up from the meadows rich with corn,
Clear in the cool September morn,
The clustered spires of Frederick stand
Green-walled by the hills of Maryland.
Round about them orchards sweep,
Apple and peach tree fruited deep,
Fair as the garden of the Lord
To the eyes of the famished rebel horde,
On that pleasant morn of the early fall
When Lee marched over the mountain-wall;
Over the mountains winding down,
Horse and foot, into Frederick town.

Forty flags with their silver stars,
Forty flags with their crimson bars,
Flapped in the morning wind: the sun
Of noon looked down, and saw not one.
Up rose old Barbara Frietchie then,

Bowed with her fourscore years and ten;
Bravest of all in Frederick town
She took up the flag the men hauled down;
In her attic window the staff she set,
To show that one heart was loyal yet.

Up the street came the rebel tread,
Stonewall Jackson riding ahead.
Under his slouched hat left and right
He glanced; the old flag met his sight.
'Halt!' – the dust-brown ranks stood fast.
'Fire!' – out blazed the rifle-blast.
It shivered the window, pane and sash;
It rent the banner with seam and gash.
Quick, as it fell, from the broken staff
Dame Barbara snatched the silken scarf.
She leaned far out on the window-sill,
And shook it forth with a royal will.
'Shoot, if you must, this old gray head,
But spare your country's flag,' she said.

A shade of sadness, a blush of shame,
Over the face of the leader came;
The nobler nature within him stirred
To life at that woman's deed and word;
'Who touches a hair of yon gray head
Dies like a dog! March on!' he said.
All day long through Frederick street
Sounded the tread of marching feet:
All day long that free flag tost
Over the heads of the rebel host.
Ever its torn folds rose and fell
On the loyal winds that loved it well;
And through the hill-gaps sunset light
Shone over it with a warm good-night.

Barbara Frietchie's work is o'er,
And the Rebel rides on his raids no more.
Honour to her! and let a tear
Fall, for her sake, on Stonewall's bier.
Over Barbara Frietchie's grave,

Flag of Freedom and Union, wave!
Peace and order and beauty draw
Round thy symbol of light and law;
And ever the stars above look down
On thy stars below in Frederick town!

EDWARD FITZGERALD

The Rubáiyát of Omar Khayyám

Awake! for Morning in the Bowl of Night
Has flung the Stone that puts the Stars to Flight:
    And Lo! the Hunter of the East has caught
The Sultán's Turret in a Noose of Light.

Dreaming when Dawn's Left Hand was in the Sky
I heard a Voice within the Tavern cry,
    'Awake, my Little ones, and fill the Cup
Before Life's Liquor in its Cup be dry.'

And, as the Cock crew, those who stood before
The Tavern shouted – 'Open then the Door!
    You know how little while we have to stay,
And, once departed, may return no more.'

Now the New Year reviving old Desires,
The thoughtful Soul to Solitude retires,
    Where the WHITE HAND OF MOSES on the Bough
Puts out, and Jesus from the Ground suspires.

Irám indeed is gone with all its Rose,
And Jamshýd's Sev'n-ring'd Cup where no one knows;
    But still the Vine her ancient Ruby yields,
And still a Garden by the Water blows.

And David's Lips are lock't; but in divine
High piping Péhlevi, with 'Wine! Wine! Wine!
    Red Wine!' – the Nightingale cries to the Rose
That yellow Cheek of her's to'incarnadine.

Come, fill the Cup, and in the Fire of Spring
The Winter Garment of Repentance fling:
   The Bird of Time has but a little way
To fly – and Lo! the Bird is on the Wing.

And look – a thousand Blossoms with the Day
Woke – and a thousand scatter'd into Clay:
   And this first Summer Month that brings the Rose
Shall take Jamshýd and Kaikobád away.

But come with old Khayyám, and leave the Lot
Of Kaikobád and Kaikhosrú forgot:
   Let Rustum lay about him as he will,
Or Hátim Tai cry Supper – heed them not.

With me along some Strip of Herbage strown
That just divides the desert from the sown,
   Where name of slave and Sultán scarce is known,
And pity Sultán Máhmúd on his Throne.

Here with a Loaf of Bread beneath the Bough,
A Flask of Wine, a Book of Verse – and Thou
   Beside me singing in the Wilderness –
And Wilderness is Paradise enow.

'How sweet is mortal Sovranty!' – think some:
Others – 'How blest the Paradise to come!'
   Ah, take the Cash in hand and wave the Rest;
Oh, the brave Music of a *distant* Drum!

Look to the Rose that blows about us – 'Lo,
Laughing,' she says, 'into the World I blow:
   At once the silken Tassel of my Purse
Tear, and its Treasure on the Garden throw.'

The Wordly Hope men set their Hearts upon
Turns Ashes – or it prospers; and anon,
   Like Snow upon the Desert's dusty Face
Lighting a little Hour or two – is gone.

And those who husbanded the Golden Grain,
And those who flung it to the Winds like Rain,
　　Alike to no such aureate Earth are turn'd
As, buried once, Men want dug up again.

Think, in this batter'd Caravanserai
Whose Doorways are alternate Night and Day,
　　How Sultán after Sultán with his Pomp
Abode his Hour or two, and went his way.

They say the Lion and the Lizard keep
The Courts where Jamshýd gloried and drank deep;
　　And Bahrám, that great Hunter – the Wild Ass
Stamps o'er his Head, and he lies fast asleep.

I sometimes think that never blows so red
The Rose as where some buried Cæsar bled;
　　That every Hyacinth the Garden wears
Dropt in its Lap from some once lovely Head.

And this delightful Herb whose tender Green
Fledges the River's Lip on which we lean –
　　Ah, lean upon it lightly! for who knows
From what once lovely Lip it springs unseen!

Ah, my Belovèd, fill the Cup that clears
TO-DAY of past Regrets and future Fears –
　　To-morrow? –Why, To-morrow I may be
Myself with Yesterday's Sev'n Thousand Years.

Lo! some we loved, the loveliest and best
That Time and Fate of all their Vintage prest,
　　Have drunk their Cup a Round or two before,
And one by one crept silently to Rest.

And we, that now make merry in the Room
They left, and Summer dresses in new Bloom,
　　Ourselves must we beneath the Couch of Earth
Descend, ourselves to make a Couch – for whom?

Ah, make the most of what we yet may spend,
Before we too into the Dust descend;
   Dust into Dust, and under Dust, to lie,
Sans Wine, sans Song, sans Singer, and – sans End!

Alike for those who for To-DAY prepare,
And those that after a To-MORROW stare,
   A Muezzín from the Tower of Darkness cries
'Fools! your Reward is neither Here nor There!'

Why, all the Saints and Sages who discuss'd
Of the Two Worlds so learnedly, are thrust
   Like foolish Prophets forth; their Words to Scorn
Are scatter'd, and their Mouths are stopt with Dust.

Oh, come with old Khayyám, and leave the Wise
To talk; one thing is certain, that Life flies;
   One thing is certain, and the Rest is Lies;
The Flower that once has blown for ever dies.

Myself when young did eagerly frequent
Doctor and Saint, and heard great Argument
   About it and about: but evermore
Came out by the same Door as in I went.

With them the Seed of Wisdom did I sow,
And with my own hand labour'd it to grow:
   And this was all the Harvest that I reap'd –
'I came like Water, and like Wind I go.'

Into this Universe, and *why* not knowing,
Nor *whence*, like Water willy-nilly flowing:
   And out of it, as Wind along the Waste,
I know not *whither*, willy-nilly blowing.

What, without asking, hither hurried *whence?*
And, without asking, *whither* hurried hence!
   Another and another Cup to drown
The Memory of this Impertinence!

Up from Earth's Centre through the Seventh Gate
I rose, and on the Throne of Saturn sate,
   And many Knots unravel'd by the Road;
But not the Knot of Human Death and Fate.

There was a Door to which I found no Key:
There was a Veil past which I could not see:
   Some little Talk awhile of ME and THEE
There seem'd – and then no more of THEE and ME.

Then to the rolling Heav'n itself I cried,
Asking, 'What Lamp had Destiny to guide
   Her little Children stumbling in the Dark?'
And – 'A blind Understanding!' Heav'n replied.

Then to this earthen Bowl did I adjourn
My Lip the secret Well of Life to learn:
   And Lip to Lip it murmur'd – 'While you live
Drink! – for once dead you never shall return.'

I think the Vessel, that with fugitive
Articulation answer'd, once did live,
   And merry-make; and the cold Lip I kiss'd
How many Kisses might it take – and give!

For in the Market-place, one Dusk of Day,
I watch'd the Potter thumping his wet Clay:
   And with its all obliterated Tongue
It murmur'd – 'Gently, Brother, gently, pray!'

Ah, fill the Cup: – what boots it to repeat
How Time is slipping underneath our Feet:
   Unborn TO-MORROW, and dead YESTERDAY,
Why fret about them if TO-DAY be sweet!

One Moment in Annihilation's Waste,
One Moment, of the Well of Life to taste –
   The Stars are setting and the Caravan
Starts for the Dawn of Nothing – Oh, make haste!

How long, how long, in infinite Pursuit
Of This and That endeavour and dispute?
    Better be merry with the fruitful Grape
Than sadden after none, or bitter, Fruit.

You know, my Friends, how long since in my House
For a new Marriage I did make Carouse:
    Divorced old barren Reason from my Bed,
And took the Daughter of the Vine to Spouse.

For 'Is' and 'Is-not' though *with* Rule and Line,
And 'Up-and-down' *without*, I could define,
    I yet in all I only cared to know,
Was never deep in anything but – Wine.

And lately, by the Tavern Door agape,
Came stealing through the Dusk an Angel Shape
    Bearing a Vessel on his Shoulder; and
He bid me taste of it; and 'twas – the Grape!

The Grape that can with Logic absolute
The Two-and-Seventy jarring Sects confute:
    The subtle Alchemist that in a Trice
Life's leaden Metal into Gold transmute.

The mighty Mahmúd, the victorious Lord,
That all the misbelieving and black Horde
    Of Fears and Sorrows that infest the Soul
Scatters and slays with his enchanted Sword.

But leave the Wise to wrangle, and with me
The Quarrel of the Universe let be:
    And, in some corner of the Hubbub coucht,
Make Game of that which makes as much of Thee.

For in and out, above, about, below,
'Tis nothing but a Magic Shadow-show,
    Play'd in a Box whose Candle is the Sun.
Round which we Phantom Figures come and go.

And if the Wine you drink, the Lip you press,
End in the Nothing all Things end in – Yes –
    Then fancy while Thou art, Thou art but what
Thou shalt be – Nothing – Thou shalt not be less.

While the Rose blows along the River Brink,
With old Khayyám the Ruby Vintage drink:
    And when the Angel with his darker Draught
Draws up to Thee – take that, and do not shrink.

'Tis all a Chequer-board of Nights and Days
Where Destiny with Men for Pieces plays:
    Hither and thither moves, and mates, and slays,
And one by one back in the Closet lays.

The Ball no Question makes of Ayes and Noes.
But Right or Left, as strikes the Player goes;
    And He that toss'd Thee down into the Field,
He knows about it all – HE knows – HE knows!

The Moving Finger writes; and, having writ,
Moves on: nor all thy Piety nor Wit
    Shall lure it back to cancel half a Line,
Nor all thy Tears wash out a Word of it.

And that inverted Bowl we call The Sky,
Whereunder crawling coop't we live and die,
    Lift not thy hands to *It* for help – for It
Rolls impotently on as Thou or I.

With Earth's first Clay They did the Last Man's knead.
And then of the Last Harvest sow'd the Seed:
    Yea, the first Morning of Creation wrote
What the Last Dawn of Reckoning shall read.

I tell Thee this – When, starting from the Goal,
Over the shoulders of the flaming Foal
    Of Heav'n Parwín and Mushtara they flung,
In my predestin'd Plot of Dust and Soul

The Vine had struck a Fibre; which about
If clings my Being – let the Súfi flout;
 Of my Base Metal may be filed a Key,
That shall unlock the Door he howls without.

And this I know: whether the one True Light,
Kindle to Love, or Wrath-consume me quite,
 One Glimpse of It within the Tavern caught
Better than in the Temple lost outright.

Oh Thou, who didst with Pitfall and with Gin
Beset the Road I was to wander in,
 Thou wilt not with Predestination round
Enmesh me, and impute my Fall to Sin?

Oh, Thou, who Man of baser Earth didst make,
And who with Eden didst devise the Snake;
 For all the Sin wherewith the Face of Man
Is blacken'd, Man's Forgiveness give – and take!

Listen again. One Evening at the Close
Of Ramazán, ere the better Moon arose,
 In that old Potter's Shop I stood alone
With the clay Population round in Rows.

And, strange to tell, among that Earthen Lot
Some could articulate, while others not:
 And suddenly one more impatient cried –
'Who *is* the Potter, pray, and who the Pot?'

Then said another – 'Surely not in vain
My Substance from the common Earth was ta'en,
 That He who subtly wrought me into Shape
Should stamp me back to common Earth again.'

Another said – 'Why, ne'er a peevish Boy,
Would break the Bowl from which he drank in Joy;
 Shall He that *made* the Vessel in pure Love
And Fancy, in an after Rage destroy!'

None answer'd this; but after Silence spake
A Vessel of a more ungainly Make:
    'They sneer at me for leaning all awry;
What! did the Hand then of the Potter shake?'

Said one – 'Folks of a surly Tapster tell,
And daub his Visage with the Smoke of Hell;
    They talk of some strict Testing of us – Pish!
He's a Good Fellow, and 'twill all be well.'

Then said another with a long-drawn Sigh,
'My Clay with long oblivion is gone dry:
    But, fill me with the old familiar Juice,
Methinks I might recover by-and-bye!'

So while the Vessels one by one were speaking,
One spied the little Crescent all were seeking:
    And then they jogg'd each other, 'Brother! Brother!
Hark to the Porter's Shoulder-knot a creaking!'

Ah, with the Grape my fading Life provide,
And wash my Body whence the Life has died,
    And in a Windingsheet of Vine-leaf wrapt,
So bury me by some sweet Garden-side.

That ev'n my buried Ashes such a Snare
Of Perfume shall fling up into the Air,
    As not a True Believer passing by
But shall be overtaken unaware.

And when Thyself with shining Foot shall pass
Among the Guests Star-scatter'd on the Grass,
    And in thy joyous Errand reach the Spot
Where I made one – turn down an empty Glass!

ALFRED, LORD TENNYSON

The Charge of the Light Brigade

Half a league, half a league,
Half a league onward,
All in the valley of Death
  Rode the six hundred.
 'Forward, the Light Brigade!
Charge for the guns!' he said.
Into the valley of Death
  Rode the six hundred.

'Forward, the Light Brigade!'
Was there a man dismayed?
Not though the soldier knew
  Some one had blundered.
Theirs not to make reply,
Theirs not to reason why,
Theirs but to do and die.
Into the valley of Death
  Rode the six hundred.

Cannon to right of them,
Cannon to left of them,
Cannon in front of them
  Volleyed and thundered;
Stormed at with shot and shell,
Boldly they rode and well,
Into the jaws of Death,
Into the mouth of Hell
  Rode the six hundred.

Flashed all the sabres bare,
Flashed as they turned in air
Sabring the gunners there,
Charging an army, while
  All the world wondered:
Plunged in the battery-smoke
Right through the line they broke;

Cossack and Russian
Reeled from the sabre-stroke
  Shattered and sundered.
Then they rode back, but not,
  Not the six hundred.

Cannon to right of them,
Cannon to left of them,
Cannon behind them
  Volleyed and thundered;
Stormed at with shot and shell,
While horse and hero fell,
They that had fought so well
Came through the jaws of Death,
Back from the mouth of Hell,
All that was left of them,
  Left of six hundred.

When can their glory fade?
O the wild charge they made!
  All the world wondered.
Honour the charge they made!
Honour the Light Brigade,
  Noble six hundred!

Ulysses

It little profits that an idle king,
By this still hearth, among these barren crags,
Matched with an agèd wife, I mete and dole
Unequal laws unto a savage race,
That hoard, and sleep, and feed, and know not me.

I cannot rest from travel: I will drink
Life to the lees: all times I have enjoyed
Greatly, have suffered greatly, both with those
That loved me, and alone; on shore, and when
Through scudding drifts the rainy Hyades
Vext the dim sea: I am become a name;

For always roaming with a hungry heart
Much have I seen and known; cities of men
And manners, climates, councils, governments,
Myself not least, but honoured of them all;
And drunk delight of battle with my peers,
Far on the ringing plains of windy Troy.
I am a part of all that I have met;
Yet all experience is an arch wherethrough
Gleams that untravelled world, whose margin fades
For ever and for ever when I move.
How dull it is to pause, to make an end,
To rust unburnished, not to shine in use!
As though to breathe were life. Life piled on life
Were all too little, and of one to me
Little remains: but every hour is saved
From that eternal silence, something more,
A bringer of new things; and vile it were
For some three suns to store and hoard myself,
And this gray spirit yearning in desire
To follow knowledge like a sinking star,
Beyond the utmost bound of human thought.

This is my son, mine own Telamachus,
To whom I leave the sceptre and the isle –
Well-loved of me, discerning to fulfil
This labour, by slow prudence to make mild
A rugged people, and through soft degrees
Subdue them to the useful and the good.
Most blameless is he, centred in the sphere
Of common duties, decent not to fail
In offices of tenderness, and pay
Meet adoration to my household gods,
When I am gone. He works his work, I mine.

There lies the port; the vessel puffs her sail:
There gloom the dark broad seas. My mariners,
Souls that have toiled, and wrought, and thought with me –
That ever with a frolic welcome took
The thunder and the sunshine, and opposed
Free hearts, free foreheads – you and I are old;
Old age hath yet his honour and his toil;

Death closes all: but something ere the end,
Some work of noble note, may yet be done,
Not unbecoming men that strove with Gods.
The lights begin to twinkle from the rocks:
The long day wanes: the slow moon climbs: the deed
Moans round with many voices. Come, my friends,
'Tis not too late to seek a newer world.
Push off, and sitting well in order smite
The sounding furrows; for my purpose holds
To sail beyond the sunset, and the baths
Of all the western stars, until I die.
It may be that the gulfs will wash us down:
It may be we shall touch the Happy Isles,
And see the great Achilles, whom we knew.
Though much is taken, much abides; and though
We are not now that strength which in old days
Moved earth and heaven, that which we are, we are;
One equal temper of heroic hearts,
Made weak by time and fate, but strong in will
To strive, to seek, to find, and not to yield.

Break, Break, Break

Break, break, break,
  On thy cold gray stones, O Sea!
And I would that my tongue could utter
  The thoughts that arise in me.

O well for the fisherman's boy,
  That he shouts with his sister at play!
O well for the sailor lad,
  That he sings in his boat on the bay!

And the stately ships go on
  To their haven under the hill;
But O for the touch of a vanished hand,
  And the sound of a voice that is still!

Break, break, break,
   At the foot of thy crags, O Sea!
But the tender grace of a day that is dead
Will never come back to me.

A Ballad of the Fleet

At Flores in the Azores Sir Richard Grenville lay,
And a pinnace, like a fluttered bird, came flying from far
      away:
'Spanish ships of war at sea! we have sighted fifty-three!'
Then sware Lord Thomas Howard: ''Fore God I am no
      coward;
But I cannot meet them here, for my ships are out of gear,
And the half my men are sick. I must fly, but follow quick.
We are six ships of the line; can we fight with fifty-three?'

Then spake Sir Richard Grenville: 'I know you are no coward;
You fly them for a moment to fight with them again.
But I've ninety men and more that are lying sick ashore.
I should count myself the coward if I left them, my Lord
      Howard,
To these Inquisition dogs and the devildoms of Spain.'

So Lord Howard passed away with five ships of war that day,
Till he melted like a cloud in the silent summer heaven;
But Sir Richard bore in hand all his sick men from the land
Very carefully and slow,
Men of Bideford in Devon,
And we laid them on the ballast down below;
For we brought them all aboard,
And they blest him in their pain, that they were not left to
      Spain,
To the thumbscrew and the stake, for the glory of the Lord.

He had only a hundred seamen to work the ship and to fight,
And he sailed away from Flores till the Spaniard came in sight,
With his huge sea-castles heaving upon the weather bow.
'Shall we fight or shall we fly?

Good Sir Richard, tell us now,
For to fight is but to die!
There'll be little of us left by the time this sun be set.'
And Sir Richard said again: 'We be all good English men.
Let us bang those dogs of Seville, the children of the devil,
For I never turned my back upon Don or devil yet.'

Sir Richard spoke and he laughed, and we roared a hurrah,
    and so
The little Revenge ran on sheer into the heart of the foe,
With her hundred fighters on deck, and her ninety sick below;
For half their fleet to the right and half to the left were seen,
And the little Revenge ran on through the long sea-lane
    between.

Thousands of their soldiers looked down from their decks and
    laughed,
Thousands of their seamen made mock at the mad little craft
Running on and on, till delayed
By their mountain-like San Philip that, of fifteen hundred tons,
And up-shadowing high above us with her yawning tiers of
    guns,
Took the breath from our sails, and we stayed.

And while now the great San Philip hung above us like a cloud
Whence the thunderbolt will fall
Long and loud,
Four galleons drew away
From the Spanish fleet that day,
And two upon the larboard and two upon the starboard lay,
And the battle thunder broke from them all.

But anon the great San Philip, she bethought herself and
    went,
Having that within her womb that had left her ill content;
And the rest they came aboard us, and they fought us hand to
    hand,
For a dozen times they came with their pikes and musqueteers,
And a dozen times we shook 'em off as a dog that shakes his
    ears

157

When he leaps from the water to the land.
And the sun went down, and the stars came out far over the
    summer sea,
But never a moment ceased the fight of the one and the
    fifty-three.
Ship after ship, the whole night long, their high-built galleons
    came,
Ship after ship, the whole night long, with her battle-thunder
    and flame;
Ship after ship, the whole night long, drew back with her
    dead and her shame.
For some were sunk and many were shattered, and so could
    fight us no more –
God of battles, was ever a battle like this in the world before?

For he said, 'Fight on! fight on!'
Though his vessel was all but a wreck;
And it chanced that, when half of the short summer night
    was gone,
With a grisly wound to be drest he had left the deck,
But a bullet struck him that was dressing it suddenly dead,
And himself he was wounded again in the side and the head,
And he said, 'Fight on! fight on!'

And the night went down and the sun smiled out far over the
    summer sea,
And the Spanish fleet with broken sides lay round us all in a
    ring;
But they dared not touch us again, for they feared that we
    still could sting,
So they watched what the end would be.
And we had not fought them in vain,
But in perilous plight were we,
Seeing forty of our poor hundred were slain,
And half of the rest of us maimed for life
In the crash of the cannonades and the desperate strife;
And the sick men down in the hold were most of them stark
    and cold,
And the pikes were all broken or bent, and the powder was
    all of it spent;
And the masts and the rigging were lying over the side;

But Sir Richard cried in his English pride:
'We have fought such a fight for a day and a night
As may never be fought again!
We have one great glory, my men!
And a day less or more
At sea or ashore,
We die – does it matter when?
Sink me the ship, Master Gunner – sink her, split her in twain!
Fall into the hands of God, not into the hands of Spain!'

And the gunner said, 'Ay, ay,' but the seamen made reply:
'We have children, we have wives,
And the Lord hath spared our lives.
We will make the Spaniard promise, if we yield, to let us go;
We shall live to fight again and to strike another blow.'
And the lion there lay dying, and they yielded to the foe.

And the stately Spanish men to their flagship bore him then,
Where they laid him by the mast, old Sir Richard caught at
    last,
And they praised him to his face with their courtly foreign
    grace;
But he rose upon their decks, and he cried:
'I have fought for Queen and Faith like a valiant man and
    true;
I have only done my duty as a man is bound to do:
With a joyful spirit I Sir Richard Grenville die!'
And he fell upon their decks and he died.

And they stared at the dead that had been so valiant and true,
And had holden the power and glory of Spain so cheap
That he dared her with one little ship and his English few;
Was he devil or man? He was devil for aught they knew,
But they sank his body with honour down into the deep,
And they manned the Revenge with a swarthier alien crew,
And away she sailed with her loss and longed for her own;
When a wind from the lands they had ruined awoke from
    sleep,
And the water began to heave and the weather to moan,
And or ever that evening ended a great gale blew,
And a wave like the wave that is raised by an earthquake grew,

Till it smote on their hulls and their sails and their masts and
    their flags,
And the whole sea plunged and fell on the shot-shattered
    navy of Spain,
And the little Revenge herself went down by the island crags
To be lost evermore in the main.

Alfred, Lord Tennyson   1809 –1892

Tears, Idle Tears

Tears, idle tears, I know not what they mean,
Tears from the depth of some divine despair
Rise in the heart, and gather to the eyes,
In looking on the happy autumn-fields,
And thinking of the days that are no more.

Fresh as the first beam glittering on a sail,
That brings our friends up from the underworld,
Sad as the last which reddens over one
That sinks with all we love below the verge;
So sad, so fresh, the days that are no more.

Ah, sad and strange as in dark summer dawns
The earliest pipe of half-awaken'd birds
To dying ears, when unto dying eyes
The casement slowly grows a glimmering square;
So sad, so strange, the days that are no more.

Dear as remember'd kisses after death,
And sweet as those by hopeless fancy feign'd
On lips that are for others; deep as love,
Deep as first love, and wild with all regret;
O Death in Life, the days that are no more!

Ring out, Wild Bells

Ring out, wild bells, to the wild sky,
    The flying cloud, the frosty light:
    The year is dying in the night;
Ring out, wild bells, and let him die.

Ring out the old, ring in the new,
    Ring, happy bells, across the snow:
    The year is going, let him go;
Ring out the false, ring in the true.

Ring out the grief that saps the mind,
    For those that here we see no more;
    Ring out the feud of rich and poor,
Ring in redress to all mankind.

Ring out a slowly dying cause,
    And ancient forms of party strife;
    Ring in the nobler modes of life,
With sweeter manners, purer laws.

Ring out the want, the care, the sin,
    The faithless coldness of the times;
    Ring out, ring out my mournful rhymes,
But ring the fuller minstrel in.

Ring out false pride in place and blood,
    The civic slander and the spite;
    Ring in the love of truth and right,
Ring in the common love of good.

Ring out old shapes of foul disease;
    Ring out the narrowing lust of gold;
    Ring out the thousand wars of old,
Ring in the thousand years of peace.

Ring in the valiant man and free,
    The larger heart, the kindlier hand;
    Ring out the darkness of the land,
Ring in the Christ that is to be.

Crossing the Bar

Sunset and evening star,
    And one clear call for me!
And may there be no moaning of the bar,
    When I put out to sea,

But such a tide as moving seems asleep,
   Too full for sound and foam,
When that which drew from out the boundless deep
   Turns again home.

Twilight and evening bell,
   And after that the dark!
And may there be no sadness of farewell,
   When I embark;

For tho' from out our bourne of Time and Place
   The flood may bear me far,
I hope to see my Pilot face to face
   When I have crost the bar.

ROBERT BROWNING

Home Thoughts from Abroad

Oh, to be in England
Now that April's there,
And whoever wakes in England
Sees, some morning, unaware,
That the lowest boughs and the brushwood sheaf
Round the elm-tree bole are in tiny leaf,
While the chaffinch sings on the orchard bough
In England – now!
And after April, when May follows,
And the whitethroat builds, and all the swallows!
Hark, where my blossomed pear-tree in the hedge
Leans to the field and scatters on the clover
Blossoms and dewdrops – at the bent spray's edge –
That's the wise thrush; he sings each song twice over,
Lest you should think he never could recapture
The first fine careless rapture!
And though the fields look rough with hoary dew
All will be gay when noontide wakes anew
The buttercups, the little children's dower
– Far brighter than this gaudy melon-flower!

Home Thoughts from the Sea

Nobly, nobly Cape Saint Vincent to the North-west died
   away;
Sunset ran, one glorious blood-red, reeking into Cadiz Bay;
Bluish 'mid the burning water, full in face Trafalgar lay;
In the dimmest North-east distance dawned Gibraltar grand
   and gray;
'Here and here did England help me: how can I help
   England?' – say,
Whoso turns as I, this evening, turn to God to praise and pray,
While Jove's planet rises yonder, silent over Africa.

How They Brought the Good News from Ghent to Aix

I sprang to the stirrup, and Joris, and he;
I galloped, Dirck galloped, we galloped all three;
'Good speed!' cried the watch, as the gate-bolts undrew;
'Speed!' echoed the wall to us galloping through;
Behind shut the postern, the lights sank to rest,
And into the midnight we galloped abreast.

Not a word to each other: we kept the great pace
Neck by neck, stride by stride, never changing our place;
I turned in my saddle and made its girths tight,
Then shortened each stirrup, and set the pique right,
Rebuckled the cheek-strap, chained slacker the bit,
Nor galloped less steadily Roland a whit.

'Twas moonset at starting; but while we drew near
Lokeren, the cocks crew and twilight dawned clear;
At Boom, a great yellow star came out to see;
At Düffeld, 'twas morning as plain as could be;
And from Mecheln church-steeple we heard the half-chime,
So Joris broke silence with, 'Yet there is time!'

At Aerschot, up leaped of a sudden the sun,
And against him the cattle stood black every one,
To stare thro' the mist at us galloping past,

And I saw my stout galloper Roland at last,
With resolute shoulders, each butting away
The haze, as some bluff river headland its spray.

And his low head and crest, just one sharp ear bent back
For my voice, and the other pricked out on his track;
And one eye's black intelligence, – ever that glance
O'er its white edge at me, his own master, askance!
And the thick heavy spume-flakes which aye and anon
His fierce lips shook upwards in galloping on.

By Hasselt, Dirck groaned; and cried Joris, 'Stay spur!
Your Roos galloped bravely, the fault's not in her,
We'll remember at Aix' – for one heard the quick wheeze
Of her chest, saw the stretched neck and staggering knees,
And sunk tail, and horrible heave of the flank,
As down on her haunches she shuddered and sank.

So we were left galloping, Joris and I,
Past Looz and past Tongres, no cloud in the sky;
The broad sun above laughed a pitiless laugh,
'Neath our feet broke the brittle bright stubble like chaff;
Till over by Dalhem a dome-spire sprang white,
And 'Gallop,' gasped Joris, 'for Aix is in sight!'

'How they'll greet us!' – and all in a moment his roan
Rolled neck and croup over, lay dead as a stone;
And there was my Roland to bear the whole weight
Of the news which alone could save Aix from her fate,
With his nostrils like pits full of blood to the brim,
And with circles of red for his eye-sockets' rim.

Then I cast loose my buffcoat, each holster let fall,
Shook off both my jack-boots, let go belt and all,
Stood up in the stirrup, leaned, patted his ear,
Called my Roland his pet-name, my horse without peer;
Clapped my hands, laughed and sang, any noise, bad or good,
Till at length into Aix Roland galloped and stood.

And all I remember is, friends flocking round
As I sat with his head 'twixt my knees on the ground;

And no voice but was praising this Roland of mine,
As I poured down his throat our last measure of wine,
Which (the burgesses voted by common consent)
Was no more than his due who brought good news from
  Ghent.

Incident of the French Camp

You know, we French stormed Ratisbon:
    A mile or so away
On a little mound, Napoleon
    Stood on our storming-day;
With neck out-thrust, you fancy how,
    Legs wide, arms locked behind,
As if to balance the prone brow
    Oppressive with its mind.

Just as perhaps he mused 'My plans
    That soar, to earth may fall,
Let once my army-leader Lannes
    Waver at yonder wall,' –
Out 'twixt the battery-smokes there flew
    A rider, bound on bound
Full-galloping; nor bridle drew
    Until he reached the mound.

Then off there flung in smiling joy,
    And held himself erect
By just his horse's mane, a boy:
    You hardly could suspect –
(So tight he kept his lips compressed,
    Scarce any blood came through)
You looked twice ere you saw his breast
    Was all but shot in two.

'Well,' cried he, 'Emperor, by God's grace
    We've got you Ratisbon!
The Marshal's in the market-place,
    And you'll be there anon

165

To see your flag-bird flap his vans
    Where I, to heart's desire,
Perched him!' The Chief's eye flashed; his plans
    Soared up again like fire.

The Chief's eye flashed; but presently
    Softened itself, as sheathes
A film the mother-eagle's eye
    When her bruised eaglet breathes:
'You're wounded!' 'Nay,' his soldier's pride
    Touched to the quick, he said:
'I'm killed, Sire!' And his Chief beside,
    Smiling the boy fell dead.

JANE M. CAMPBELL

We Plough the Fields

We plough the fields, and scatter
    The good seed on the land,
But it is fed and watered
    By God's almighty hand:
He sends the snow in winter,
    The warmth to swell the grain,
The breezes and the sunshine,
    And soft refreshing rain:

> *All good gifts around us*
>   *Are sent from heaven above;*
> *Then thank the Lord, O thank the Lord,*
>   *For all his love.*

He only is the maker
    Of all things near and far,
He paints the wayside flower,
    He lights the evening star.
The winds and waves obey him,
    By him the birds are fed;
Much more to us, his children,
    He gives our daily bread:

We thank thee then, O Father,
    For all things bright and good;
The seed-time and the harvest,
    Our life, our health, our food.
No gifts have we to offer
    For all thy love imparts,
But that which thou desirest,
    Our humble, thankful hearts:

> *All good gifts around us*
>   *Are sent from heaven above;*
> *Then thank the Lord, O thank the Lord,*
>   *For all his love.*

EMILY BRONTË

The Old Stoic

Riches I hold in light esteem,
And Love I laugh to scorn;
And lust of Fame was but a dream
That vanished with the morn –

And if I pray, the only prayer
That moves my lips for me
Is – 'Leave the heart that now I bear,
And give me liberty.'

Yes, as my swift days near their goal,
'Tis all that I implore –
Through life and death, a chainless soul,
With courage to endure!

WALT WHITMAN

O Captain! My Captain!

O Captain! my Captain! our fearful trip is done,
The ship has weather'd every rack, the prize we sought is won,
The port is near, the bells I hear, the people all exulting,
While follow eyes the steady keel, the vessel grim and daring;
But O heart! heart! heart!
O the bleeding drops of red,
Where on the deck my Captain lies,
Fallen cold and dead.

O Captain! my Captain! rise up and hear the bells;
Rise up – for you the flag is flung – for you the bugle trills,
For you bouquets and ribbon'd wreaths – for you the shores
a-crowding,
For you they call, the swaying mass, their eager faces turning;
Here Captain! dear father!
This arm beneath your head!
It is some dream that on the deck,
You've fallen cold and dead.

My Captain does not answer, his lips are pale and still,
My father does not feel my arm, he has no pulse nor will,
The ship is anchor'd safe and sound, its voyage closed and done,
From fearful trip the victor ship comes in with object won:
Exult O shores, and ring O bells!
But I with mournful tread,
Walk the deck my Captain lies,
Fallen cold and dead.

CHARLES KINGSLEY

The Three Fishers

Three fishers went sailing away to the West,
Away to the West as the sun went down;
Each thought on the woman who loved him the best,
And the children stood watching them out of the town;

For men must work, and women must weep,
And there's little to earn, and many to keep,
    Though the harbour bar be moaning.

Three wives sat up in the lighthouse tower,
  And they trimmed the lamps as the sun went down;
They looked at the squall, and they looked at the shower,
  And the night-rack came rolling up ragged and brown.
  But men must work, and women must weep,
  Though storms be sudden, and waters deep,
    And the harbour bar be moaning.

Three corpses lay out on the shining sands
  In the morning gleam as the tide went down,
And the women are weeping and wringing their hands
  For those who will never come home to the town;
  For men must work, and women must weep,
  And the sooner it's over, the sooner to sleep;
    And good-bye to the bar and its moaning.

Ode to the North-east Wind

Welcome, wild North-easter.
  Shame it is to see
Odes to every zephyr;
  Ne'er a verse to thee.
Welcome, black North-easter!
  O'er the German foam;
O'er the Danish moorlands,
  From thy frozen home.
Tired we are of summer,
  Tired of gaudy glare,
Showers soft and streaming,
  Hot and breathless air.
Tired of listless dreaming,
  Through the lazy day:
Jovial wind of winter,
  Turn us out to play!
Sweep the golden reed-beds;
  Crisp the lazy dyke;

169

Hunger into madness
   Every plunging pike.
Fill the lake with wild-fowl;
   Fill the marsh with snipe;
While on dreary moorlands
   Lonely curlew pipe.
Through the black fir-forest
   Thunder harsh and dry,
Shattering down the snow-flakes
   Off the curdled sky.
Hark! The brave North-easter!
   Breast-high lies the scent,
On by holt and headland,
   Over heath and bent.
Chime, ye dappled darlings,
   Through the sleet and snow.
Who can over-ride you?
   Let the horses go!
Chime, ye dappled darlings,
   Down the roaring blast;
You shall see a fox die
   Ere an hour be past.
Go! and rest to-morrow,
   Hunting in your dreams,
While our skates are ringing
   O'er the frozen streams.
Let the luscious South-wind
   Breathe in lovers' sighs,
While the lazy gallants
   Bask in ladies' eyes.
What does he but soften
   Heart alike and pen?
'Tis the hard grey weather
   Breeds hard English men.
What's the soft South-wester?
   'Tis the ladies' breeze,
Bringing home their true-loves
   Out of all the seas:
But the black North-easter,
   Through the snowstorm hurled,

Drives our English hearts of oak
   Seaward round the world.
Come, as came our fathers,
   Heralded by thee,
Conquering from the eastward,
   Lords by land and sea.
Come; and strong within us
   Stir the Viking's blood;
Bracing brain and sinew;
   Blow, thou wind of God!

The Sands of Dee

'O Mary, go and call the cattle home,
   And call the cattle home,
   And call the cattle home
  Across the sands of Dee;'
The western wind was wild and dank with foam,
  And all alone went she.

The western tide crept up along the sand,
   And o'er and o'er the sand,
   And round and round the sand,
  As far as eye could see.
The rolling mist came down and hid the land:
  And never home came she.

'Oh! is it weed, or fish, or floating hair –
   A tress of golden hair,
   A drownèd maiden's hair
  Above the nets at sea?
Was never salmon yet that shone so fair
  Among the stakes on Dee.'

They rowed her in across the rolling foam,
   The cruel crawling foam,
   The cruel hungry foam,
  To her grave beside the sea:
But still the boatman hear her call the cattle home
  Across the sands of Dee.

Young and Old

When all the world is young, lad,
  And all the trees are green;
And every goose a swan, lad,
  And every lass a queen;
Then hey for boot and horse, lad,
  And round the world away;
Young blood must have its course, lad,
  And every dog his day.

When all the world is old, lad,
  And all the trees are brown;
And all the sport is stale, lad,
  And all the wheels run down;
Creep home, and take your place there,
  The spent and maimed among:
God grant you find one face there,
  You loved when all was young.

A. H. CLOUGH

Say Not the Struggle Naught Availeth

Say not the struggle nought availeth,
  The labour and the wounds are vain,
The enemy faints not, nor faileth,
  And as things have been, they remain.

If hopes were dupes, fears may be liars;
  It may be, in yon smoke concealed,
Your comrades chase e'en now the fliers,
  And, but for you, possess the field.

For while the tired waves, vainly breaking,
  Seem here no painful inch to gain,
Far back through creeks and inlets making
  Comes, silent, flooding in, the main,

And not by eastern windows only,
   When daylight comes, comes in the light,
In front the sun climbs slow, how slowly,
   But westward, look, the land is bright.

JULIA WARD HOWE

Battle Hymn of the Republic

Mine eyes have seen the glory of the coming of the Lord;
He is trampling out the vintage where the grapes of wrath are
   stored;
He hath loosed the fatal lightning of his terrible swift sword:
  His Truth is marching on.

I have seen him in the watch-fires of a hundred circling camps;
They have builded him an altar in the evening dews and damps;
I have read his righteous sentence by the dim and flaring lamps:
  His Day is marching on.

I have read a fiery gospel, writ in burnished rows of steel:
'As you deal with my contemners, so with you my grace shall
   deal;'
Let the Hero born of woman crush the serpent with his heel,
  Since God is marching on.

He has sounded forth the trumpet that shall never call retreat;
He is sifting out the hearts of men before his judgment-seat;
O be swift, my soul, to answer him; be jubilant, my feet!
  Our God is marching on.

In the beauty of the lilies Christ was born across the sea,
With a glory in his bosom that transfigures you and me;
As he died to make men holy, let us die to make men free,
  While God is marching on.

He is coming like the glory of the morning on the wave;
He is wisdom to the mighty, he is succour to the brave;
So the world shall be his footstool, and the soul of time his
   slave:
  Our God is marching on.

JAMES RUSSELL LOWELL

Once to Every Man and Nation

Once to every man and nation
  Comes the moment to decide,
In the strife of truth with falsehood,
  For the good or evil side:
Some great cause, God's new Messiah,
  Offering each the bloom or blight;
And the choice goes by for ever
  'Twixt that darkness and that light.

Then to side with truth is noble,
  When we share her wretched crust,
Ere her cause bring fame and profit,
  And 'tis prosperous to be just;
Then it is the brave man chooses,
  While the coward stands aside,
Till the multitude make virtue
  Of the faith they had denied.

By the light of burning martyrs,
  Christ, thy bleeding feet we track,
Toiling up new Calvaries ever
  With the cross that turns not back.
New occasions teach new duties;
  Time makes ancient good uncouth;
They must upward still and onward
  Who would keep abreast of truth.

Though the cause of evil prosper,
  Yet 'tis truth alone is strong;
Though her portion be the scaffold,
  And upon the throne be wrong,
Yet that scaffold sways the future,
  And, behind the dim unknown,
Standeth God within the shadow,
  Keeping watch above his own.

DION BOUCICAULT

The Wearing of the Green

O Paddy dear, and did you hear the news that's going round?
The shamrock is forbid by law to grow on Irish ground;
St. Patrick's Day no more we'll keep, his colours can't be
    seen,
For there's a bloody law again the wearing of the Green.
I met with Napper Tandy, and he took me by the hand,
And he said, 'How's poor old Ireland, and how does she stand?'
She's the most distressful country that ever yet was seen,
They are hanging men and women for the wearing of the
    Green.

Then since the colour we must wear is England's cruel Red,
Sure Ireland's sons will ne'er forget the blood that they have
    shed.
You may take the shamrock from your hat and cast it on the
    sod,
But 'twill take root and flourish there, though under foot 'tis
    trod.
When law can stop the blades of grass from growing as they
    grow,
And when the leaves in summer-time their verdure dare not
    show,
Then I will change the colour that I wear in my caubeen,
But till that day, please God, I'll stick to wearing of the Green.

But if at last our colour should be torn from Ireland's heart,
Her sons with shame and sorrow from the dear old isle will
    part;
I've heard a whisper of a country that lies beyond the sea,
Where rich and poor stand equal in the light of freedom's day.
O Erin, must we leave you, driven by a tyrant's hand?
Must we ask a mother's blessing from a strange and distant
    land?
Where the cruel cross of England shall nevermore be seen,
And where, please God, we'll live and die still wearing of the
    Green.

S. JOHNSON

City of God

City of God, how broad and far
  Outspread thy walls sublime!
The true thy chartered freemen are
  Of every age and clime.

One holy Church, one army strong,
  One steadfast, high intent;
One working band, one harvest-song,
  One King omnipotent.

How purely hath thy speech come down
  From man's primeval youth!
How grandly hath thine empire grown
  Of freedom, love, and truth!

How gleam thy watch-fires through the night
  With never-fainting ray!
How rise thy towers, serene and bright,
  To meet the dawning day!

In vain the surge's angry shock,
  In vain the drifting sands:
Unharmed upon the eternal Rock
  The eternal City stands.

MATTHEW ARNOLD

The Forsaken Merman

Come, dear children, let us away;
Down and away below.
Now my brothers call from the bay;
Now the great winds shorewards blow;
Now the salt tides seawards flow;

Now the wild white horses play,
Champ and chafe and toss in the spray.
Children dear, let us away.
This way, this way.

Call her once before you go.
Call once yet.
In a voice that she will know:
'Margaret! Margaret!'
Children's voices should be dear
(Call once more) to a mother's ear:
Children's voices, wild with pain.
Surely she will come again.
Call her once and come away.
This way, this way.
'Mother dear, we cannot stay.'
The wild white horses foam and fret.
Margaret! Margaret!

Come, dear children, come away down.
Call no more.
One last look at the white-wall'd town,
And the little grey church on the windy shore.
Then come down.
She will not come though you call all day.
Come away, come away.

Children dear, was it yesterday
We heard the sweet bells over the bay?
In the caverns where we lay,
Through the surf and through the swell,
The far-off sound of a silver bell?
Sand-strewn caverns, cool and deep,
Where the winds are all asleep;
Where the spent lights quiver and gleam;
Where the salt weed sways in the stream;
Where the sea-beasts rang'd all round
Feed in the ooze of their pasture-ground;
Where the sea-snakes coil and twine,
Dry their mail and bask in the brine;
Where great whales come sailing by,

Sail and sail, with unshut eye,
Round the world for ever and aye?
When did music come this way?
Children dear, was it yesterday?

Children dear, was it yesterday
(Call yet once) that she went away?
Once she sate with you and me,
On a red gold throne in the heart of the sea,
And the youngest sate on her knee.
She comb'd its bright hair, and she tended it well,
When down swung the sound of the far-off bell.
She sigh'd, she look'd up through the clear green sea.
She said; 'I must go, for my kinsfolk pray
In the little grey church on the shore to-day.
'Twill be Easter-time in the world – ah me!
And I lose my poor soul, Merman, here with thee.'
I said; 'Go up, dear heart, through the waves;
Say thy prayer, and come back to the kind sea-caves.'
She smil'd, she went up through the surf in the bay.
Children dear, was it yesterday?

   Children dear, were we long alone?
'The sea grows stormy, the little ones moan.
Long prayers,' I said, 'in the world they say.
Come,' I said, and we rose through the surf in the bay.
We went up the beach, by the sandy down
Where the sea-stocks bloom, to the white-wall'd town.
Through the narrow pav'd streets, where all was still,
To the little grey church on the windy hill.
From the church came a murmur of folk at their prayers,
But we stood without in the cold blowing airs.
We climb'd on the graves, on the stones, worn with rains,
And we gaz'd up the aisle through the small leaded panes.
She sate by the pillar; we saw her clear:
'Margaret, hist! come quick, we are here.
Dear heart,' I said, 'we are long alone.
The sea grows stormy, the little ones moan.'
But, ah, she gave me never a look,
For her eyes were seal'd to the holy book.

Loud prays the priest; shut stands the door.
Come away, children, call no more.
Come away, come down, call no more.

   Down, down, down.
Down to the depths of the sea.
She sits at her wheel in the humming town,
Singing most joyfully.
Hark, what she sings; 'O joy, O joy,
For the humming street, and the child with its toy.
For the priest, and the bell, and the holy well.
For the wheel where I spun,
And the blessed light of the sun.'
And so she sings her fill,
Singing most joyfully,
Till the shuttle falls from her hand,
And the whizzing wheel stands still.
She steals to the window, and looks at the sand;
And over the sand at the sea;
And her eyes are set in a stare;
And anon there breaks a sigh,
And anon there drops a tear,
From a sorrow-clouded eye,
And a heart sorrow-laden,
A long, long sigh,
For the cold strange eyes of a little Mermaiden,
And the gleam of her golden hair.

   Come away, away children.
Come children, come down.
The hoarse wind blows colder;
Lights shine in the town.
She will start from her slumber
When gusts shake the door;
She will hear the winds howling,
Will hear the waves roar.
We shall see, while above us
The waves roar and whirl,
A ceiling of amber,
A pavement of pearl.
Singing, 'Here came a mortal,

But faithless was she.
And alone dwell for ever
The kings of the sea.'

But, children, at midnight,
When soft the winds blow;
When clear falls the moonlight;
When spring-tides are low:
When sweet airs come seaward
From heaths starr'd with broom;
And high rocks throw mildly
On the blanch'd sands a gloom:
Up the still, glistening beaches,
Up the creeks we will hie;
Over banks of bright seaweed
The ebb-tide leaves dry.
We will gaze, from the sand-hills,
At the white, sleeping town;
At the church on the hill-side –
    And then come back down.
Singing, 'There dwells a lov'd one,
But cruel is she.
She left lonely for ever
The kings of the sea.'

W. J. CORY

Heraclitus

They told me, Heraclitus, they told me you were dead;
They brought me bitter news to hear and bitter tears to shed.
I wept, as I remembered, how often you and I
Had tired the sun with talking and sent him down the sky.

And now that thou art lying, my dear old Carian guest,
A handful of grey ashes, long long ago at rest,
Still are thy pleasant voices, thy nightingales, awake,
For Death, he taketh all away, but them he cannot take.

The Two Captains

When George the Third was reigning a hundred years ago,
He ordered Captain Farmer to chase the foreign foe.
'You're not afraid of shot,' said he, 'you're not afraid of wreck,
So cruise about the west of France in the frigate called *Quebec*.

Quebec was once a Frenchman's town, but twenty years ago
King George the Second sent a man called General Wolfe,
    you know,
To clamber up a precipice and look into Quebec,
As you'd look down a hatchway when standing on the deck.

If Wolfe could beat the Frenchmen then so you can beat them
    now.
Before he got inside the town he died, I must allow.
But since the town was won for us it is a lucky name,
And you'll remember Wolfe's good work, and you shall do
    the same.'

Then Farmer said, 'I'll try, sir,' and Farmer bowed so low
That George could see his pigtail tied in a velvet bow.
George gave him his commission, and that it might be safer,
Signed 'King of Britain, King of France,' and sealed it with
    a wafer.

Then proud was Captain Farmer in a frigate of his own,
And grander on his quarter-deck than George upon the throne.
He'd two guns in his cabin, and on the spar-deck ten,
And twenty on the gun-deck, and more than ten score men.

And as a huntsman scours the brakes with sixteen brace of dogs,
With two-and-thirty cannon the ship explored the fogs.
From Cape la Hogue to Ushant, from Rochefort to Belleisle,
She hunted game till reef and mud were rubbing on her keel.

The fogs are dried, the frigate's side is bright with melting tar,
The lad up in the foretop sees square white sails afar;
The east wind drives three square-sailed masts from out the
    Breton bay,
And 'Clear for action!' Farmer shouts, and reefers yell 'Hooray!'

The Frenchmen's captain had a name I wish I could pro-
nounce;
A Breton gentleman was he, and wholly free from bounce,
One like those famous fellows who died by guillotine
For honour and the fleurs-de-lys and Antoinette the Queen.

The Catholic for Louis, the Protestant for George,
Each captain drew as bright a sword as saintly smiths could
forge;
And both were simple seamen, but both could understand
How each was bound to win or die for flag and native land.

The French ship was *la Surveillante*, which means the watchful
maid;
She folded up her head-dress and began to cannonade.
Her hull was clean, and ours was foul; we had to spread more
sail.
On canvas, stays, and topsail yards her bullets came like hail.

Sore smitten were both captains, and many lads beside,
And still to cut our rigging the foreign gunners tried.
A sail-clad spar came flapping down athwart a blazing gun;
We could not quench the rushing flames, and so the French-
man won.

Our quarter-deck was crowded, the waist was all aglow;
Men hung upon the taffrail, half scorched but loth to go;
Our captain sat where once he stood, and would not quit his
chair.
He bade his comrades leap for life, and leave him bleeding
there.

The guns were hushed on either side, the Frenchmen lowered
boats,
They flung us planks and hencoops, and everything that floats.
They risked their lives, good fellows! to bring their rivals aid.
'Twas by the conflagration the peace was strangely made.

La Surveillante was like a sieve; the victors had no rest.
They had to dodge the east wind to reach the port of Brest,

And where the waves leapt lower, and the riddled ship went
    slower,
In triumph, yet in funeral guise, came fisher-boats to tow her.

They dealt with us as brethren, they mourned for Farmer dead;
And as the wounded captives passed each Breton bowed the
    head.
Then spoke the French Lieutenant, "Twas fire that won, not
    we.
You never struck your flag to us; you'll go to England free.'

'Twas the sixth day of October, seventeen hundred seventy-
    nine,
A year when nations ventured against us to combine,
Quebec was burnt and Farmer slain, by us remembered not;
But thanks be to the French book wherein they're not forgot.

Now you, if you've to fight the French, my youngster, bear in
    mind
Those seamen of King Louis so chivalrous and kind;
Think of the Breton gentlemen who took our lads to Brest,
And treat some rescued Breton as a comrade and a guest.

CECIL FRANCES ALEXANDER

All Things Bright and Beautiful

All things bright and beautiful,
    All creatures great and small,
All things wise and wonderful,
    The Lord God made them all.

Each little flower that opens,
    Each little bird that sings,
He made their glowing colours,
    He made their tiny wings:

The purple-headed mountain,
    The river running by,
The sunset and the morning,
    That brightens up the sky:

The cold wind in the winter,
　　The pleasant summer sun,
The ripe fruits in the garden,
　　He made them every one:

The tall trees in the greenwood,
　　The meadows for our play,
The rushes by the water
　　To gather every day:

He gave us eyes to see them,
　　And lips that we might tell
How great is God Almighty,
　　Who has made all things well.

WILLIAM WHITING

Eternal Father, Strong to Save

Eternal Father, strong to save,
Whose arm doth bind the restless wave,
Who bidd'st the mighty ocean deep
Its own appointed limits keep:
　　O hear us when we cry to thee
　　For those in peril on the sea.

O Saviour, whose almighty word
The winds and waves submissive heard,
Who walkedst on the foaming deep,
And calm amid its rage didst sleep:
　　O hear us when we cry to thee
　　For those in peril on the sea.

O sacred Spirit, who didst brood
Upon the chaos dark and rude,
Who bad'st its angry tumult cease,
And gavest light and life and peace:
　　O hear us when we cry to thee
　　For those in peril on the sea.

O Trinity of love and power,
  Our brethren shield in danger's hour;
From rock and tempest, fire and foe,
Protect them wheresoe'er they go:
    And ever let there rise to thee
    Glad hymns of praise from land and sea.

JOHN ELLERTON

The Day Thou Gavest

The day thou gavest, Lord, is ended,
  The darkness falls at thy behest;
To thee our morning hymns ascended,
  Thy praise shall sanctify our rest.

We thank thee that thy Church unsleeping,
  While earth rolls onward into light,
Through all the world her watch is keeping,
  And rests not now by day or night.

As o'er each continent and island
  The dawn leads on another day,
The voice of prayer is never silent,
  Nor dies the strain of praise away.

The sun that bids us rest is waking
  Our brethren 'neath the western sky,
And hour by hour fresh lips are making
  Thy wondrous doings heard on high.

So be it, Lord; thy throne shall never,
  Like earth's proud empires, pass away;
Thy kingdom stands, and grows for ever,
  Till all thy creatures own thy sway.

H. C. WORK

Marching through Georgia

Bring the good old bugle, boys, we'll sing another song,
Sing it with a spirit that will start the world along,
Sing it as we used to sing it, fifty thousand strong,
 While we were marching through Georgia.
   Hurrah! hurrah! we bring the jubilee!
   Hurrah! hurrah! the flag that makes you free!
   So we sang the chorus from Atlanta to the sea,
   While we were marching through Georgia.

How the darkies shouted when they heard the joyful sound;
How the turkeys gobbled which our commissary found;
How the sweet potatoes even started from the ground,
 While we were marching through Georgia.
   Hurrah! etc.

Yes, and there were Union men who wept with joyful tears,
When they saw the honoured flag they had not seen for years;
Hardly could they be restrained from breaking forth in cheers,
 While we were marching through Georgia.
   Hurrah! etc.

'Sherman's dashing Yankee boys will never reach the coast,'
So the saucy rebels said, and 'twas a handsome boast;
Had they not forgot, alas, to reckon with the host,
 While we were marching through Georgia.
   Hurrah! etc.

So we made a thoroughfare for Freedom and her train,
Sixty miles in latitude, three hundred to the main;
Treason fled before us, for resistance was in vain,
 While we were marching through Georgia.
   Hurrah! etc.

SABINE BARING-GOULD

Onward, Christian Soldiers

Onward, Christian soldiers!
  Marching as to war,
With the cross of Jesus
  Going on before.
Christ the royal Master
  Leads against the foe;
Forward into battle,
  See, his banners go:
        Onward, Christian soldiers,
          Marching as to war,
        With the cross of Jesus
          Going on before.

At the sign of triumph
  Satan's legions flee;
On then, Christian soldiers,
  On to victory!
Hell's foundations quiver
  At the shout of praise;
Brothers, lift your voices,
  Loud your anthems raise:

Like a mighty army
  Moves the Church of God;
Brothers, we are treading
  Where the saints have trod;
We are not divided,
  All one body we,
One in hope and doctrine,
  One in charity:

Crowns and thrones may perish,
  Kingdoms rise and wane,
But the Church of Jesus
  Constant will remain;
Gates of hell can never
  'Gainst that Church prevail;

We have Christ's own promise,
   And that cannot fail:

Onward, then, ye people,
   Join our happy throng,
Blend with ours your voices
   In the triumph song;
Glory, laud, and honour
   Unto Christ the King;
This through countless ages
   Men and angels sing:
        Onward, Christian soldiers,
        Marching as to war,
        With the cross of Jesus
        Going on before.

Through the Night of Doubt and Sorrow

Through the night of doubt and sorrow
   Onward goes the pilgrim band,
Singing songs of expectation,
   Marching to the Promised Land.

Clear before us through the darkness
   Gleams and burns the guiding light;
Brother clasps the hand of brother,
   Stepping fearless through the night.

One the light of God's own presence
   O'er his ransomed people shed,
Chasing far the gloom and terror,
   Brightening all the path we tread;

One the object of our journey,
   One the faith which never tires,
One the earnest looking forward,
   One the hope our God inspires:

One the strain that lips of thousands
   Lift as from the heart of one;

One the conflict, one the peril,
　　One the march in God begun;

One the gladness of rejoicing
　　On the far eternal shore,
Where the one almighty Father
　　Reigns in love for evermore.

ALFRED AUSTIN

Is Life Worth Living?

Is life worth living? Yes, so long
　　As Spring revives the year,
And hails us with the cuckoo's song,
　　To show that she is here;
So long as May of April takes
　　In smiles and tears farewell,
And windflowers dapple all the brakes,
　　And primroses the dell;
While children in the woodlands yet
　　Adorn their little laps
With ladysmock and violet,
　　And daisy-chain their caps;
While over orchard daffodils
　　Cloud-shadows float and fleet,
And ousel pipes and laverock trills,
　　And young lambs buck and bleat;
So long as that which bursts the bud
　　And swells and tunes the rill
Makes springtime in the maiden's blood,
　　Life is worth living still.

Life not worth living! Come with me,
　　Now that, through vanishing veil,
Shimmers the dew on lawn and lea,
　　And milk foams in the pail;
Now that June's sweltering sunlight bathes
　　With sweat the striplings lithe,

As fall the long straight scented swathes
  Over the crescent scythe;
Now that the throstle never stops
  His self-sufficing strain,
And woodbine-trails festoon the copse,
  And eglantine the lane;
Now rustic labour seems as sweet
  As leisure, and blithe herds
Wend homeward with unweary feet,
  Carolling like the birds;
Now all, except the lover's vow,
  And nightingale, is still;
Here, in the twilight hour, allow,
  Life is worth living still.

When Summer, lingering half-forlorn,
  On Autumn loves to lean,
And fields of slowly yellowing corn
  Are girt by woods still green;
When hazel-nuts wax brown and plump,
  And apples rosy-red,
And the owlet hoots from hollow stump,
  And the dormouse makes its bed;
When crammed are all the granary floors
  And the Hunter's moon is bright,
And life again is sweet indoors,
  And logs again alight;
Ay, even when the houseless wind
  Waileth through cleft and chink,
And in the twilight maids grow kind,
  And jugs are filled and clink;
When children clasp their hands and pray
  'Be done Thy Heavenly will!'
Who doth not lift his voice, and say,
  'Life is worth living still'?

Is life worth living? Yes, so long
  As there is wrong to right,
Wail of the weak against the strong,
  Or tyranny to fight;

Long as there lingers gloom to chase,
    Or streaming tear to dry,
One kindred woe, one sorrowing face
    That smiles as we draw nigh;
Long as at tale of anguish swells
    The heart, and lids grow wet,
And at the sound of Christmas bells
    We pardon and forget;
So long as Faith with Freedom reigns,
    And loyal Hope survives,
And gracious Charity remains
    To leaven lowly lives;
While there is one untrodden tract
    For Intellect or Will,
And men are free to think and act,
    Life is worth living still.

Not care to live while English homes
    Nestle in English trees,
And England's Trident-Sceptre roams
    Her territorial seas!
Not live while English songs are sung
    Wherever blows the wind,
And England's laws and England's tongue
    Enfranchise half mankind!
So long as in Pacific main
    Or on Atlantic strand,
Our kin transmit the parent strain,
    And love the Mother-land;
So long as flashes English steel,
    And English trumpets shrill,
He is dead already who doth not feel
    Life is worth living still.

W. CHATTERTON DIX

As with Gladness Men of Old

As with gladness men of old
Did the guiding star behold,
As with joy they hailed its light,
Leading onward, beaming bright,
So, most gracious God, may we
Evermore be led to thee.

As with joyful steps they sped
To that lowly manager-bed,
There to bend the knee before
Him whom heaven and earth adore,
So may we with willing feet
Ever seek thy mercy-seat.

As they offered gifts most rare
At that manger rude and bare,
So may we with holy joy,
Pure, and free from sin's alloy,
All our costliest treasures bring,
Christ, to thee our heavenly King.

Holy Jesus, every day
Keep us in the narrow way;
And, when earthly things are past,
Bring our ransomed souls at last
Where they need no star to guide,
Where no clouds thy glory hide.

In the heavenly country bright
Need they no created light;
Thou its light, its joy, its crown,
Thou its sun which goes not down:
There for ever may we sing
Alleluyas to our King.

A. C. SWINBURNE

The Garden of Proserpine

Here, where the world is quiet;
  Here, where all trouble seems
Dead winds' and spent waves' riot
  In doubtful dreams of dreams;
I watch the green field growing
For reaping folk and sowing,
For harvest-time and mowing,
  A sleepy world of streams.

I am tired of tears and laughter,
  And men that laugh and weep;
Of what may come hereafter
  For men that sow to reap:
I am weary of days and hours,
Blown buds of barren flowers,
Desires and dreams and powers
  And everything but sleep.

Here life has death for neighbour,
  And far from eye or ear
Wan waves and wet winds labour,
  Weak ships and spirits steer;
They drive adrift, and whither
They wot not who make thither;
But no such winds blow hither,
  And no such things grow here.

No growth of moor or coppice,
  No heather-flower or vine,
But bloomless buds of poppies,
  Green grapes of Proserpine,
Pale beds of blowing rushes
Where no leaf blooms or blushes
Save this whereout she crushes
  For dead men deadly wine.

Pale, without name or number,
  In fruitless fields of corn,

They bow themselves and slumber
  All night till light is born;
And like a soul belated,
In hell and heaven unmated,
By cloud and mist abated
  Comes out of darkness morn.

Though one were strong as seven,
  He too with death shall dwell,
Nor wake with wings in heaven,
  Nor weep for pains in hell;
Though one were fair as roses,
His beauty clouds and closes;
And well though love reposes,
  In the end it is not well.

Pale, beyond porch and portal,
  Crowned with calm leaves, she stands
Who gathers all things mortal
  With cold immortal hands;
Her languid lips are sweeter
Than love's who fears to greet her
To men that mix and meet her
  From many times and lands.

She waits for each and other,
  She waits for all men born;
Forgets the earth her mother,
  The life of fruits and corn;
And spring and seed and swallow
Take wing for her and follow
Where summer song rings hollow
  And flowers are put to scorn.

There go the loves that wither,
  The old loves with wearier wings;
And all dead years draw thither,
  And all disastrous things;
Dead dreams of days forsaken,
Blind buds that snows have shaken,
Wild leaves that winds have taken,
  Red strays of ruined springs.

We are not sure of sorrow,
   And joy was never sure;
To-day will die to-morrow;
   Time stoops to no man's lure;
And love, grown faint and fretful,
With lips but half regretful
Sighs, and with eyes forgetful
   Weeps that no loves endure.

From too much love of living,
   From hope and fear set free,
We thank with brief thanksgiving
   Whatever gods may be
That no life lives for ever;
That dead men rise up never;
That even the weariest river
   Winds somewhere safe to sea.

Then star nor sun shall waken,
   Nor any change of light:
Nor sound of waters shaken,
   Nor any sound or sight:
Nor wintry leaves nor vernal,
Nor days nor things diurnal;
Only the sleep eternal
   In an eternal night.

JOHN DAVIDSON

The Runnable Stag

When the pods went pop on the broom, green broom,
   And apples began to be golden-skinned,
We harboured a stag in the Priory coomb,
   And we feathered his trail up-wind, up-wind,
   We feathered his trail up-wind –
     A stag of warrant, a stag, a stag,
     A runnable stag, a kingly crop,
    Brow, bay and tray and three on top,
     A stag, a runnable stag.

Then the huntsman's horn rang yap, yap, yap,
    And 'Forwards' we heard the harbourer shout;
But 'twas only a brocket that broke a gap
    In the beechen underwood, driven out,
    From the underwood antlered out
        By warrant and might of the stag, the stag,
        The runnable stag, whose lordly mind
        Was bent on sleep, though beamed and tined
        He stood, a runnable stag.

So we tufted the covert till afternoon
    With Tinkerman's Pup and Bell-of-the-North;
And hunters were sulky and hounds out of tune
    Before we tufted the right stag forth,
    Before we tufted him forth,
        The stag of warrant, the wily stag,
        The runnable stag with his kingly crop,
        Brow, bay and tray and three on top,
        The royal and runnable stag.

It was Bell-of-the-North and Tinkerman's Pup
    That stuck to the scent till the copse was drawn.
'Tally ho! tally ho!' and the hunt was up,
    The tufters whipped and the pack laid on,
    The resolute pack laid on,
        And the stag of warrant away at last,
        The runnable stag, the same, the same,
        His hoofs on fire, his horns like flame,
        A stag, a runnable stag.

'Let your gelding be: if you check or chide
    He stumbles at once and you're out of the hunt;
For three hundred gentlemen, able to ride,
    On hunters accustomed to bear the brunt,
    Accustomed to bear the brunt,
        Are after the runnable stag, the stag,
        The runnable stag with his kingly crop,
        Brow, bay and tray and three on top,
        The right, the runnable stag.'

By perilous paths in coomb and dell,
    The heather, the rocks, and the river-bed,

The pace grew hot, for the scent lay well,
  And a runnable stag goes right ahead,
  The quarry went right ahead –
    Ahead, ahead, and fast and far;
    His antlered crest, his cloven hoof,
    Brow, bay and tray and three aloof,
    The stag, the runnable stag.

For a matter of twenty miles and more,
  By the densest hedge and the highest wall,
Through herds of bullocks he baffled the lore
  Of harbourer, huntsman, hounds and all,
  Of harbourer, hounds and all –
    The stag of warrant, the wily stag,
    For twenty miles, and five and five,
    He ran, and he never was caught alive,
    This stag, this runnable stag.

When he turned at bay in the leafy gloom,
  In the emerald gloom where the brook ran deep,
He heard in the distance the rollers boom,
  And he saw in a vision of peaceful sleep,
  In a wonderful vision of sleep,
    A stag of warrant, a stag, a stag,
    A runnable stag in a jewelled bed,
    Under the sheltering ocean dead,
    A stag, a runnable stag.

So a fateful hope lit up his eye,
  And he opened his nostrils wide again,
And he tossed his branching antlers high
  As he headed the hunt down the Charlock glen,
  As he raced down the echoing glen
    For five miles more, the stag, the stag,
    For twenty miles, and five and five,
    Not to be caught now, dead or alive,
    The stag, the runnable stag.

Three hundred gentlemen, able to ride,
  Three hundred horses as gallant and free,

Beheld him escape on the evening tide,
　Far out till he sank in the Severn Sea,
　Till he sank in the depths of the sea –
　　The stag, the buoyant stag, the stag
　　That slept at last in a jewelled bed
　　Under the sheltering ocean spread,
　　The stag, the runnable stag.

AUSTIN DOBSON

A Ballade of the Armada

King Philip had vaunted his claims;
He had sworn for a year he would sack us;
With an army of heathenish names
He was coming to fagot and stack us;
Like the thieves of the sea he would track us,
And shatter our ships on the main;
But we had bold Neptune to back us –
And where are the galleons of Spain?

His carackes were christened of dames
To the kirtles whereof he would tack us;
With his saints and his gilded stern-frames
He had thought like an egg-shell to crack us;
Now Howard may get to his Flaccus,
And Drake to his Devon again,
And Hawkins bowl rubbers to Bacchus –
For where are the galleons of Spain?

Let his Majesty hang to St. James
The axe that he whetted to hack us;
He must play at some lustier games
Or at sea he can hope to our-thwack us;
To his mines of Peru he would pack us
To tug at his bullet and chain;
Alas! that his Greatness should lack us! –
But where are the galleons of Spain?

Gloriana! – the Don may attack us
Whenever his stomach be fain;
He must reach us before he can rack us, . . .
And where are the galleons of Spain?

WILFRID S. BLUNT

The Old Squire

I like the hunting of the hare
    Better than that of the fox;
I like the joyous morning air,
    And the crowing of the cocks.

I like the calm of the early fields,
    The ducks asleep by the lake,
The quiet hour which Nature yields,
    Before mankind is awake.

I like the pheasants and feeding things
    Of the unsuspicious morn;
I like the flap of the wood-pigeon's wings
    As she rises from the corn.

I like the blackbird's shriek, and his rush
    From the turnips as I pass by,
And the partridge hiding her head in a bush
    For her young ones cannot fly.

I like these things, and I like to ride
    When all the world is in bed,
To the top of the hill where the sky grows wide,
    And where the sun grows red.

The beagles at my horse heels trot,
    In silence after me;
There's Ruby, Roger, Diamond, Dot,
    Old Slut and Margery, –

A score of names well used, and dear,
  The names my childhood knew;
The horn, with which I rouse their cheer,
  Is the horn my father blew.

I like the hunting of the hare
  Better than that of the fox;
The new world still is all less fair
  Than the old world it mocks.

I covet not a wider range
  Than these dear manors give;
I take my pleasures without change,
  And as I lived I live.

I leave my neighbours to their thought;
  My choice it is, and pride,
On my own lands to find my sport,
  In my own fields to ride.

The hare herself no better loves
  The field where she was bred,
Than I the habit of these groves,
  My own inherited.

I know my quarries every one,
  The meuse where she sits low;
The road she chose to-day was run
  A hundred years ago.

The lags, the gills, the forest ways,
  The hedgerows one and all,
These are the kingdoms of my chase,
  And bounded by my wall;

Nor has the world a better thing,
  Though one should search it round,
Than thus to live one's own sole king,
  Upon one's own sole ground.

I like the hunting of the hare;
   It brings me, day by day,
The memory of old days as fair,
   With dead men past away.

To these, as homeward still I ply
   And pass the churchyard gate,
Where all are laid as I must lie,
   I stop and raise my hat.

I like the hunting of the hare;
   New sports I hold in scorn.
I like to be as my fathers were,
   In the days e'er I was born.

A. C. AINGER

God Is Working His Purpose out

God is working his purpose out as year succeeds to year;
God is working his purpose out and the time is drawing near;
Nearer and nearer draws the time, the time that shall surely be,
When the earth shall be filled with the glory of God as the
    waters cover the sea.

From utmost east to utmost west where'er man's foot hath
    trod,
By the mouth of many messengers goes forth the voice of God,
'Give ear to me, ye continents, ye isles, give ear to me,
That the earth may be filled with the glory of God as the
    waters cover the sea.'

What can we do to work God's work, to prosper and increase
The brotherhood of all mankind, the reign of the Prince of
    Peace?
What can we do to hasten the time, the time that shall surely
    be,
When the earth shall be filled with the glory of God as the
    waters cover the sea?

March we forth in the strengths of God with the banner of
    Christ unfurled,
That the light of the glorious gospel of truth may shine
    throughout the world;
Fight we the fight with sorrow and sin, to set their captives
    free,
That the earth may be filled with the glory of God as the
    waters cover the sea.

All we can do is nothing worth unless God blesses the deed;
Vainly we hope for the harvest-tide till God gives life to the
    seed;
Yet nearer and nearer draws the time, the time that shall
    surely be,
When the earth shall be filled with the glory of God as the
    waters cover the sea.

ARTHUR O'SHAUGHNESSY

Ode

We are the music makers,
  And we are the dreamers of dreams,
Wandering by lone sea-breakers,
  And sitting by desolate streams; –
World-losers and world-forsakers,
  On whom the pale moon gleams:
Yet we are the movers and shakers
  Of the world for ever, it seems.

With wonderful deathless ditties
We build up the world's great cities,
  And out of a fabulous story
  We fashion an empire's glory:
One man with a dream, at pleasure,
  Shall go forth and conquer a crown;
And three with a new song's measure
  Can trample a kingdom down.

We, in the ages lying
　In the buried past of the earth,
Built Nineveh with our sighing,
　And Babel itself in our mirth;
And o'erthrew them with prophesying
　To the old of the new world's worth;
For each age is a dream that is dying,
　Or one that is coming to birth.

A breath of our inspiration
Is the life of each generation;
　A wondrous thing of our dreaming
　Unearthly, impossible seeming –
The soldier, the king, and the peasant
　Are working together in one,
Till our dream shall become their present,
　And their work in the world be done.

They had no vision amazing
Of the goodly house they are raising;
　They had no divine foreshowing
　Of the land to which they are going:
But on one man's soul it hath broken,
　A light that doth not depart;
And his look, or a word he hath spoken,
　Wrought flame in another man's heart.

And therefore to-day is thrilling
With a past day's late fulfilling;
　And the multitudes are enlisted
　In the faith that their fathers resisted,
And, scorning the dream of to-morrow,
　Are bringing to pass, as they may,
In the world, for its joy or its sorrow,
　The dream that was scorned yesterday.

But we, with our dreaming and singing,
　Ceaseless and sorrowless we!
The glory about us clinging
　Of the glorious futures we see,
Our souls with high music ringing:
　O men! it must ever be

That we dwell, in our dreaming and singing,
  A little apart from ye.

For we are afar with the dawning
  And the suns that are not yet high,
And out of the infinite morning
  Intrepid you hear us cry –
How, spite of your human scorning,
  Once more God's future draws nigh,
And already goes forth the warning
  That ye of the past must die.

Great hail! we cry to the comers
  From the dazzling unknown shore;
Bring us hither your sun and your summers,
  And renew our world as of yore;
You shall teach us your song's new numbers,
  And things that we dreamed not before:
Yea, in spite of a dreamer who slumbers,
  And a singer who sings no more.

W. E. HENLEY

Invictus

Out of the night that covers me,
  Black as the pit from pole to pole,
I thank whatever gods may be
  For my unconquerable soul.

In the fell clutch of circumstance
  I have not winced nor cried aloud.
Under the bludgeonings of chance
  My head is bloody, but unbowed.

Beyond this place of wrath and tears
  Looms but the Horror of the shade,
And yet the menace of the years
  Finds, and shall find, me unafraid.

It matters not how strait the gate,
    How charged with punishments the scroll,
I am the master of my fate:
    I am the captain of my soul.

R. L. STEVENSON

Requiem

Under the wide and starry sky,
Dig the grave and let me lie.
Glad did I live and gladly die,
    And I laid me down with a will.

This be the verse you grave for me:
Here he lies where he longed to be;
Home is the sailor, home from sea,
    And the hunter home from the hill.

FRANCIS THOMPSON

The Kingdom of God

O world invisible, we view thee,
O world intangible, we touch thee,
O world unknowable, we know thee,
Inapprehensible, we clutch thee!

Does the fish soar to find the ocean,
The eagle plunge to find the air –
That we ask of the stars in motion
If they have rumour of thee there?

Not where the wheeling systems darken,
And our benumbed conceiving soars! –
The drift of pinions, would we hearken,
Beats at our own clay-shuttered doors.

The angels keep their ancient places; –
Turn but a stone, and start a wing!
'Tis ye, 'tis your estrangèd faces,
That miss the many-splendoured thing.

But (when so sad thou canst not sadder)
Cry; – and upon thy so sore loss
Shall shine the traffic of Jacob's ladder
Pitched betwixt Heaven and Charing Cross.

Yea, in the night, my Soul, my daughter,
Cry, – clinging Heaven by the hems;
And lo, Christ walking on the water,
Not of Gennesareth, but Thames!

A. E. HOUSMAN

1887

From Clee to heaven the beacon burns,
  The shires have seen it plain,
From north and south the sign returns
  And beacons burn again.

Look left, look right, the hills are bright,
  The dales are light between,
Because 'tis fifty years to-night
  That God has saved the Queen.

Now, when the flame they watch not towers
  About the soil they trod,
Lads, we'll remember friends of ours
  Who shared the work with God.

To skies that knit their heartstrings right,
  To fields that bred them brave,
The saviours come not home to-night:
  Themselves they could not save.

It dawns in Asia, tombstones show
  And Shropshire names are read;
And the Nile spills his overflow
  Beside the Severn's dead.

We pledge in peace by farm and town
  The Queen they served in war,
And fire the beacons up and down
  The land they perished for.

'God save the Queen' we living sing,
  From height to height 'tis heard;
And with the rest your voices ring,
  Lads of the Fifty-third.

Oh, God will save her, fear you not:
  Be you the men you've been,
Get you the sons your fathers got,
  And God will save the Queen.

The Recruit

Leave your home behind, lad,
  And reach your friends your hand,
And go, and luck go with you
  While Ludlow tower shall stand.

Oh, come you home of Sunday
  When Ludlow streets are still
And Ludlow bells are calling
  To farm and lane and mill,

Or come you home of Monday
  When Ludlow market hums
And Ludlow chimes are playing
  'The conquering hero comes',

Come you home a hero,
  Or come not home at all,

The lads you leave will mind you
    Till Ludlow tower shall fall.

And you will list the bugle
    That blows in lands of morn,
And make the foes of England
    Be sorry you were born.

And you till trump of doomsday
    On lands of morn may lie,
And make the hearts of comrades
    Be heavy where you die.

Leave your home behind you,
    Your friends by field and town:
Oh, town and field will mind you
    Till Ludlow tower is down.

SIR HENRY NEWBOLT

Drake's Drum

Drake he's in his hammock an' a thousand mile away,
    (Capten, art tha sleepin' there below?),
Slung atween the round shot in Nombre Dios Bay,
    An' dreamin' arl the time o' Plymouth Hoe.
Yarnder lumes the Island, yarnder lie the ships,
    Wi' sailor lads a dancin' heel-an'-toe,
An' the shore-lights flashin', an' the night-tide dashin',
    He sees et arl so plainly as he saw et long ago.

Drake he was a Devon man, an' rüled the Devon seas,
    (Capten, art tha sleepin' there below?),
Rovin' tho' his death fell, he went wi' heart at ease,
    An' dreamin' arl the time o' Plymouth Hoe.
'Take my drum to England, hang et by the shore,
    Strike et when your powder's runnin' low;
If the Dons sight Devon, I'll quit the port o' Heaven,
    An' drum them up the Channel as we drummed them
        long ago.'

Drake he's in his hammock till the great Armadas come,
  (Capten, art tha sleepin' there below?),
Slung atween the round shot, listenin' for the drum,
  An' dreamin' arl the time o' Plymouth Hoe.
Call him on the deep sea, call him up the Sound,
  Call him when ye sail to meet the foe;
Where the old trades' plyin' an' the old flag flyin'
  They shall find him ware an' wakin', as they found him long
    ago!

Admirals All

Effingham, Grenville, Raleigh, Drake,
  Here's to the bold and free!
Benbow, Collingwood, Byron, Blake,
  Hail to the Kings of the Sea!
Admirals all, for England's sake,
  Honour be yours and fame!
And honour, as long as waves shall break,
  To Nelson's peerless name!

Admirals all, for England's sake,
  Honour be yours and fame!
And honour, as long as waves shall break,
  To Nelson's peerless name!

Essex was fretting in Cadiz Bay
  With the galleons fair in sight;
Howard at last must give him his way,
  And the word was passed to fight.
Never was schoolboy gayer than he,
  Since holidays first began:
He tossed his bonnet to wind and sea,
  And under the guns he ran.

Drake nor devil nor Spaniard feared,
  Their cities he put to the sack;
He singed his Catholic Majesty's beard,
  And harried his ships to wrack.

209

He was playing at Plymouth a rubber of bowls
  When the great Armada came;
But he said, 'They must wait their turn, good souls,'
  And he stooped, and finished the game.

Fifteen sail were the Dutchmen bold,
  Duncan he had but two:
But he anchored them fast where the Texel shoaled
  And his colours aloft he flew.
'I've taken the depth to a fathom,' he cried,
  'And I'll sink with a right good will,
For I know when we're all of us under the tide,
  My flag will be fluttering still.'

Splinters were flying above, below,
  When Nelson sailed the Sound:
'Mark you, I wouldn't be elsewhere now,'
  Said he, 'for a thousand pound!'
The Admiral's signal bade him fly,
  But he wickedly wagged his head,
He clapped the glass to his sightless eye
  And 'I'm damned if I see it,' he said.

Admirals all, they said their say
  (The echoes are ringing still),
Admirals all, they went their way
  To the haven under the hill.
But they left us a kingdom none can take,
  The realm of the circling sea,
To be ruled by the rightful sons of Blake
  And the Rodneys yet to be.

  Admirals all, for England's sake,
    Honour be yours and fame!
  And honour, as long as waves shall break,
    To Nelson's peerless name!

He Fell among Thieves

'Ye have robbed,' said he, 'ye have slaughtered and made
  an end,
  Take your ill-got plunder, and bury the dead:
What will ye more of your guest and sometime friend?'
  'Blood for our blood,' they said.

He laughed: 'If one may settle the score for five,
  I am ready; but let the reckoning stand till day:
I have loved the sunlight as dearly as any alive.'
  'You shall die at dawn,' said they.

He flung his empty revolver down the slope,
  He climbed alone to the Eastward edge of the trees;
All night long in a dream untroubled of hope
  He brooded, clasping his knees.

He did not hear the monotonous roar that fills
  The ravine where the Yassin river sullenly flows;
He did not see the starlight on the Laspur hills,
  Or the far Afghan snows.

He saw the April noon on his books aglow,
  The wistaria trailing in at the window wide;
He heard his father's voice from the terrace below
  Calling him down to ride.

He saw the gray little church across the park,
  The mounds that hide the loved and honoured dead;
The Norman arch, the chancel softly dark,
  The brasses black and red.

He saw the School Close, sunny and green,
  The runner beside him, the stand by the parapet wall,
The distant tape, and the crowd roaring between
  His own name over all.

He saw the dark wainscot and timbered roof,
  The long tables, and the faces merry and keen;
The College Eight and their trainer dining aloof,
  The Dons on the daïs serene.

211

He watched the liner's stem ploughing the foam,
    He felt her trembling speed and the thrash of her screw;
He heard her passengers' voices talking of home,
    He saw the flag she flew.

And now it was dawn. He rose strong on his feet,
    And strode to his ruined camp below the wood;
He drank the breath of the morning cool and sweet;
    His murderers round him stood.

Light on the Laspur hills was broadening fast,
    The blood-red snow-peaks chilled to a dazzling white:
He turned, and saw the golden circle at last,
    Cut by the Eastern height.

'O glorious Life, Who dwellest in earth and sun,
    I have lived, I praise and adore Thee.'

                                        A sword swept.

Over the pass the voices one by one
    Faded, and the hill slept.

Vitaï Lampada

There's a breathless hush in the Close to-night –
    Ten to make and the match to win –
A bumping pitch and a blinding light,
    An hour to play and the last man in.
And it's not for the sake of a ribboned coat,
    Or the selfish hope of a season's fame,
But his Captain's hand on his shoulder smote –
    'Play up! play up! and play the game!'

The sand of the desert is sodden red, –
    Red with the wreck of a square that broke; –
The Gatling's jammed and the Colonel dead,
    And the regiment blind with dust and smoke.
The river of death has brimmed his banks,
    And England's far, and Honour a name,
But the voice of a schoolboy rallies the ranks:
    'Play up! play up! and play the game!'

This is the word that year by year,
  While in her place the School is set,
Every one of her sons must hear,
  And none that hears it dare forget.
This they all with a joyful mind
  Bear through life like a torch in flame,
And falling fling to the host behind –
  'Play up! play up! and play the game!'

Ireland, Ireland

Down thy valleys, Ireland, Ireland,
  Down thy valleys green and sad,
Still thy spirit wanders wailing,
  Wanders wailing, wanders mad.

Long ago that anguish took thee,
  Ireland, Ireland, green and fair,
Spoilers strong in darkness took thee,
  Broke thy heart and left thee there.

Down thy valleys, Ireland, Ireland,
  Still thy spirit wanders mad;
All too late they love that wronged thee,
  Ireland, Ireland, green and sad.

A. C. BENSON

Land of Hope and Glory

Dear Land of Hope, thy hope is crowned.
  God make thee mightier yet!
On Sov'ran brows, beloved, renowned,
  Once more thy crown is set.
Thine equal laws, by Freedom gained,
  Have ruled thee well and long;
By Freedom gained, by Truth maintained,
  Thine Empire shall be strong.

Land of Hope and Glory, Mother of the Free,
How shall we extol thee, who are born of thee?
Wider still and wider shall thy bounds be set;
God, who made thee mighty, make thee mightier yet.

Thy fame is ancient as the days,
    As Ocean large and wide;
A pride that dares, and heeds not praise,
    A stern and silent pride:
Not that false joy that dreams content
    With what our sires have won;
The blood a hero sire hath spent
    Still nerves a hero son.
        Land of Hope and Glory, etc.

W. B. YEATS

Easter 1916

I have met them at close of day
Coming with vivid faces
From counter or desk among grey
Eighteenth-century houses.
I have passed with a nod of the head
Or polite meaningless words,
Or have lingered awhile and said
Polite meaningless words,
And thought before I had done
Of a mocking tale or a gibe
To please a companion
Around the fire at the club,
Being certain that they and I
But lived where motley is worn:
All changed, changed utterly:
A terrible beauty is born.

That woman's days were spent
In ignorant good-will,
Her nights in argument
Until her voice grew shrill.

What voice more sweet than hers
When, young and beautiful,
She rode to harriers?
This man had kept a school
And rode our wingèd horse;
This other his helper and friend
Was coming into his force;
He might have won fame in the end,
So sensitive his nature seemed,
So daring and sweet his thought.
This other man I had dreamed
A drunken, vainglorious lout.
He had done most bitter wrong
To some who are near my heart,
Yet I number him in the song;
He, too, has resigned his part
In the casual comedy;
He, too, has been changed in his turn,
Transformed utterly:
A terrible beauty is born.

Hearts with one purpose alone
Through summer and winter seem
Enchanted to a stone
To trouble the living stream.
The horse that comes from the road,
The rider, the birds that range
From cloud to tumbling cloud,
Minute by minute they change;
A shadow of cloud on the stream
Changes minute by minute;
A horse-hoof slides on the brim,
And a horse plashes within it;
The long-legged moor-hens dive,
And hens to moor-cocks call;
Minute by minute they live:
The stone's in the midst of all.

Too long a sacrifice
Can make a stone of the heart.
O when may it suffice?

That is Heaven's part, our part
To murmur name upon name,
As a mother names her child
When sleep at last has come
On limbs that had run wild.
What is it but nightfall?
No, no, not night but death;
Was it needless death after all?
For England may keep faith
For all that is done and said.
We know their dream; enough
To know they dreamed and are dead;
And what if excess of love
Bewildered them till they died?
I write it out in a verse –
MacDonagh and MacBride
And Connolly and Pearse
Now and in time to be,
Whatever green is worn,
Are changed, changed utterly:
A terrible beauty is born.

The Lake Isle of Innisfree

I will arise and go now, and go to Innisfree,
And a small cabin build there, of clay and wattles made:
Nine bean-rows will I have there, a hive for the honey-bee,
And live alone in the bee-loud glade.

And I shall have some peace there, for peace comes dropping
    slow,
Dropping from the veils of the morning to where the cricket
    sings;
There midnight's all a glimmer, and noon a purple glow,
And evening full of the linnet's wings.

I will arise and go now, for always night and day
I hear lake water lapping with low sounds by the shore;
While I stand on the roadway, or on the pavements grey,
I hear it in the deep heart's core.

RUDYARD KIPLING

The Ballad of East and West

Oh, East is East, and West is West, and never the twain shall meet,
Till Earth and Sky stand presently at God's great Judgement Seat;
But there is neither East nor West, Border, nor Breed, nor Birth,
When two strong men stand face to face, though they come from the
*   ends of the earth!*

Kamal is out with twenty men to raise the Border-side,
And he has lifted the Colonel's mare that is the Colonel's
        pride.
He has lifted her out of the stable-door between the dawn and
        the day,
And turned the calkins upon her feet, and ridden her far
        away.
Then up and spoke the Colonel's son that led a troop of the
        Guides:
'Is there never a man of all my men can say where Kamal
        hides?'
Then up and spoke Mohammed Khan, the son of the
        Ressaldar:
'If ye know the track of the morning-mist, ye know where
        his pickets are.
At dusk he harries the Abazai – at dawn he is into Bonair,
But he must go by Fort Bukloh to his own place to fare.
So if ye gallop to Fort Bukloh as fast as a bird can fly,
By the favour of God ye may cut him off ere he win to the
        Tongue of Jagai.
But if he be past the Tongue of Jagai, right swiftly turn ye
        then,
For the length and the breadth of that grisly plain is sown
        with Kamal's men.
There is rock to the left, and rock to the right, and low lean
        thorn between,
And ye may hear a breech-bolt snick where never a man is
        seen.'
The Colonel's son has taken horse, and a raw rough dun was
        he,

217

With the mouth of a bell and the heart of Hell and the head
    of a gallows-tree.
The Colonel's son to the Fort has won, they bid him stay to
    eat –
Who rides at the tail of a Border thief, he sits not long at his
    meat.
He's up and away from Fort Bukloh as fast as he can fly,
Till he was aware of his father's mare in the gut of the Tongue
    of Jagai,
Till he was aware of his father's mare with Kamal upon her
    back,
And when he could spy the white of her eye, he made the
    pistol crack.
He has fired once, he has fired twice, but the whistling ball
    went wide.
'Ye shoot like a soldier,' Kamal said. 'Show now if ye can
    ride!'
It's up and over the Tongue of Jagai, as blown dust-devils
    go,
The dun he fled like a stag of ten, but the mare like a barren
    doe.
The dun he leaned against the bit and slugged his head above,
But the red mare played with the snaffle-bars, as a maiden
    plays with a glove.
There was rock to the left and rock to the right, and low lean
    thorn between,
And thrice he heard a breech-bolt snick tho' never a man was
    seen.
They have ridden the low moon out of the sky, their hoofs
    drum up the dawn,
The dun he went like a wounded bull, but the mare like a
    new-roused fawn.
The dun he fell at a water-course – in a woeful heap fell he,
And Kamal has turned the red mare back, and pulled the rider
    free.
He has knocked the pistol out of his hand – small room was
    there to strive,
' 'Twas only by favour of mine,' quoth he, 'ye rode so long
    alive:
There was not a rock for twenty mile, there was not a clump
    of tree,

But covered a man of my own men with his rifle cocked on
  his knee.
If I had raised my bridle-hand, as I have held it low,
The little jackals that flee so fast were feasting all in a row.
If I had bowed my head on my breast, as I have held it high,
The kite that whistles above us now were gorged till she
  could not fly.'
Lightly answered the Colonel's son: 'Do good to bird and
  beast,
But count who come for the broken meats before thou
  makest a feast.
If there should follow a thousand swords to carry my bones
  away,
Belike the price of a jackal's meal were more than a thief
  could pay.
They will feed their horse on the standing crop, their men on
  the garnered grain.
The thatch of the byres will serve their fires when all the
  cattle are slain.
But if thou thinkest the price be fair, – thy brethren wait to
  sup,
The hound is kin to the jackal-spawn, – howl, dog, and call
  them up!
And if thou thinkest the price be high, in steer and gear and
  stack,
Give me my father's mare again, and I'll fight my own way
  back!'
Kamal has gripped him by the hand and set him upon his
  feet.
'No talk shall be of dogs,' said he, 'when wolf and grey wolf
  meet.
May I eat dirt if thou hast hurt of me in deed or breath;
What dam of lances brought thee forth to jest at the dawn
  with Death?'
Lightly answered the Colonel's son: 'I hold by the blood of
  my clan:
Take up the mare for my father's gift – by God, she has
  carried a man!'
The red mare ran to the Colonel's son, and nuzzled against
  his breast;

'We be two strong men,' said Kamal then, 'but she loveth
  the younger best.
So she shall go with a lifter's dower, my turquoise-studded
  rein,
My 'broidered saddle and saddle-cloth, and silver stirrups
  twain.'
The Colonel's son a pistol drew, and held it muzzle-end,
'Ye have taken the one from a foe,' said he. 'Will ye take the
  mate from a friend?'
'A gift for a gift,' said Kamal straight; 'a limb for the risk of
  a limb.
Thy father has sent his son to me, I'll send my son to him!'
With that he whistled his only son, that dropped from a
  mountain-crest –
He trod the ling like a buck in spring, and he looked like a
  lance in rest.
'Now here is thy master,' Kamal said, 'who leads a troop of
  the Guides,
And thou must ride at his left side as shield on shoulder rides.
Till Death or I cut loose the tie, at camp and board and bed,
Thy life is his – thy fate it is to guard him with thy head.
So, thou must eat the White Queen's meat, and all her foes
  are thine,
And thou must harry thy father's hold for the peace of the
  Border-line.
And thou must make a trooper tough and hack thy way to
  power –
Belike they will raise thee to Ressaldar when I am hanged in
  Peshawur!'

They have looked each other between the eyes, and there they
  found no fault.
They have taken the Oath of the Brother-in-Blood on
  leavened bread and salt:
They have taken the Oath of the Brother-in-Blood on fire
  and fresh-cut sod,
On the hilt and the haft of the Khyber knife, and the
  Wondrous Names of God.
The Colonel's son he rides the mare and Kamal's boy the dun,
And two have come back to Fort Bukloh where there went
  forth but one.

And when they drew to the Quarter-Guard, full twenty
    swords flew clear –
There was not a man but carried his feud with the blood of
    the mountaineer.
'Ha' done! ha' done!' said the Colonel's son. 'Put up the steel
    at your sides!
Last night ye had struck at a Border thief – to-night 'tis a man
    of the Guides!'

Oh, East is East, and West is West, and never the twain shall
    meet,
Till Earth and Sky stand presently at God's great Judgment Seat;
But there is neither East nor West, Border, nor Breed, nor Birth,
When two strong men stand face to face, though they come from
    the ends of the earth!

Recessional

1897

God of our fathers, known of old,
    Lord of our far-flung battle-line,
Beneath whose awful Hand we hold
    Dominion over palm and pine –
Lord God of Hosts, be with us yet,
Lest we forget – lest we forget!

The tumult and the shouting dies;
    The Captains and the Kings depart:
Still stands Thine ancient sacrifice,
    An humble and a contrite heart.
Lord God of Hosts, be with us yet,
Lest we forget – lest we forget!

Far-called, our navies melt away;
    On dune and headland sinks the fire:
Lo, all our pomp of yesterday
    Is one with Nineveh and Tyre!
Judge of the Nations, spare us yet,
Lest we forget – lest we forget!

If, drunk with sight of power, we loose
   Wild tongues that have not Thee in awe,
Such boastings as the Gentiles use,
   Or lesser breeds without the Law –
Lord God of Hosts, be with us yet,
Lest we forget – lest we forget!

For heathen heart that puts her trust
   In reeking tube and iron shard,
All valiant dust that builds on dust,
   And guarding, calls not Thee to guard,
For frantic boast and foolish word –
Thy mercy on Thy People, Lord!

For All We Have and Are

1914

For all we have and are,
For all our children's fate,
Stand up and take the war.
The Hun is at the gate!
Our world has passed away,
In wantonness o'erthrown.
There is nothing left to-day
But steel and fire and stone!
      Though all we knew depart,
      The old Commandments stand: –
      'In courage keep your heart,
      In strength lift up your hand.'

Once more we hear the word
That sickened earth of old: –
'No law except the Sword
Unsheathed and uncontrolled.'
Once more it knits mankind,
Once more the nations go
To meet and break and bind
A crazed and driven foe.

Comfort, content, delight,
The ages' slow-bought gain,
They shrivelled in a night.
Only ourselves remain
To face the naked days
In silent fortitude,
Through perils and dismays
Renewed and re-renewed.
Though all we made depart,
The old Commandments stand: –
'In patience keep your heart,
In strength lift up your hand.'

No easy hope or lies
Shall bring us to our goal,
But iron sacrifice
Of body, will, and soul.
There is but one task for all –
One life for each to give.
What stands if Freedom fall?
Who dies if England live?

Danny Deever

'What are the bugles blowin' for?' said Files-on-Parade.
'To turn you out, to turn you out,' the Colour-Sergeant said.
'What makes you look so white, so white?' said Files-on-
    Parade.
'I'm dreadin' what I've got to watch,' the Colour-Sergeant
    said.
    For they're hangin' Danny Deever, you can hear the
      Dead March play,
    The Regiment's in 'ollow square – they're hangin' him
      to-day;
    They've taken of his buttons off an' cut his stripes away,
    An' they're hangin' Danny Deever in the mornin'.

'What makes the rear-rank breathe so 'ard?' said Files-on-
    Parade.
'It's bitter cold, it's bitter cold,' the Colour-Sergeant said.

'What makes that front-rank man fall down?' said Files-on-
    Parade.
'A touch o' sun, a touch o' sun,' the Colour-Sergeant said.
    They are hangin' Danny Deever, they are marchin' of 'im
        round,
    They 'ave 'alted Danny Deever by 'is coffin on the
        ground;
    An' 'e'll swing in 'arf a minute for a sneakin' shootin'
        hound –
    O they're hangin' Danny Deever in the mornin'!

' 'Is cot was right-'and cot to mine,' said Files-on-Parade.
' 'E's sleepin' out an' far to-night,' the Colour-Sergeant said.
'I've drunk 'is beer a score o' times,' said Files-on-Parade.
' 'E's drinkin' bitter beer alone,' the Colour-Sergeant said.
    They are hangin' Danny Deever, you must mark 'im to
        'is place,
    For 'e shot a comrade sleepin' – you must look 'im in the
        face;
    Nine 'undred of 'is county an' the Regiment's disgrace,
    While they're hangin' Danny Deever in the mornin'.

'What's that so black agin the sun?' said Files-on-Parade.
'It's Danny fightin' 'ard for life,' the Colour-Sergeant said.
'What's that that whimpers over'ead?' said Files-on-Parade.
'It's Danny's soul that's passin' now,' the Colour-Sergeant
        said.
    For they're done with Danny Deever, you can 'ear the
        quickstep play,
    The Regiment's in column, an' they're marchin' us away;
    Ho! the young recruits are shakin', an' they'll want their
        beer to-day,
    After hangin' Danny Deever in the mornin'!

Tommy

I went into a public-'ouse to get a pint o' beer,
The publican 'e up an' sez, 'We serve no red-coats here.'
The girls be'ind the bar they laughed an' giggled fit to die,
I outs into the street again an' to myself sez I:

O it's Tommy this, an' Tommy that, an' 'Tommy, go
    away';
But it's 'Thank you, Mister Atkins,' when the band begins
    to play –
The band begins to play, my boys, the band begins to play,
O it's 'Thank you, Mister Atkins,' when the band begins to
    play.

I went into a theatre as sober as could be,
They gave a drunk civilian room, but 'adn't none for me;
They sent me to the gallery or round the music-'alls,
But when it comes to fightin', Lord! they'll shove me in the
    stalls!
    For it's Tommy this, an' Tommy that, an' 'Tommy, wait
        outside';
    But it's 'Special train for Atkins' when the trooper's on the
        tide –
    The troopship's on the tide, my boys, the troopship's on
        the tide,
    O it's 'Special train for Atkins' when the trooper's on the
        tide.

Yes, makin' mock o' uniforms that guard you while you sleep
Is cheaper than them uniforms, an' they're starvation cheap;
An' hustlin' drunken soldiers when they're goin' large a bit
Is five times better business than paradin' in full kit.
    Then it's Tommy this, an' Tommy that, an' 'Tommy,
        'ow's yer soul?'
    But it's 'Thin red line of 'eroes' when the drums begin to
        roll –
    The drums begin to roll, my boys, the drums begin to roll,
    O it's 'Thin red line of 'eroes' when the drums begin to
        roll.

We aren't no thin red 'eroes, nor we aren't no blackguards
    too,
But single men in barricks, most remarkable like you;
An' if sometimes our conduck isn't all your fancy paints,
Why, single men in barricks don't grow into plaster saints;
    While it's Tommy this, an' Tommy that, an' 'Tommy, fall
        be'ind,'

But it's 'Please to walk in front, sir,' when there's trouble
   in the wind –
There's trouble in the wind, my boys, there's trouble in the
   wind,
O it's 'Please to walk in front, sir,' when there's trouble in
   the wind.

You talk o' better food for us, an' schools, an' fires, an' all:
We'll wait for extry rations if you treat us rational.
Don't mess about the cook-room slops, but prove it to our
   face
The Widow's Uniform is not the soldier-man's disgrace.
   For it's Tommy this, an' Tommy that, an' 'Chuck him out,
      the brute!'
   But it's 'Saviour of 'is country' when the guns begin to
      shoot;
   An' it's Tommy this, an' Tommy that, an' anything you
      please;
   An' Tommy ain't a bloomin' fool – you bet that Tommy
      sees!

Boots

We're foot – slog – slog – slog – sloggin' over Africa –
Foot – foot – foot – foot – sloggin' over Africa –
(Boots – boots – boots – boots – movin' up and down again!)
         There's no discharge in the war!

Seven – six – eleven – five – nine-an'-twenty mile to-day –
Four – eleven – seventeen – thirty-two the day before –
(Boots – boots – boots – boots – movin' up and down again!)
         There's no discharge in the war!

Don't – don't – don't – don't – look at what's in front of you.
(Boots – boots – boots – boots – movin' up an' down again);
Men – men – men – men – men go mad with watchin' 'em,
         An' there's no discharge in the war!

Try – try – try – try – to think o' something different –
Oh – my – God – keep – me from goin' lunatic!

(Boots – boots – boots – boots – movin' up an' down again!)
            There's no discharge in the war!

Count – count – count – count – the bullets in the bandoliers.
If – your – eyes – drop – they will get atop o' you!
(Boots – boots – boots – boots – movin' up and down again) –
            There's no discharge in the war!

We – can – stick – out – 'unger, thirst, an' weariness,
But – not – not – not – not the chronic sight of 'em –
Boots – boots – boots – boots – movin' up an' down again,
            An' there's no discharge in the war!

'T'ain't – so – bad – by – day because o' company,
But night – brings – long – strings – o' forty thousand million
Boots – boots – boots – boots – movin' up an' down again.
            There's no discharge in the war!

I – 'ave – marched – six – weeks in 'Ell an' certify
It – is – not – fire – devils, dark or anything,
But boots – boots – boots – boots – movin' up an' down again,
            An' there's no discharge in the war!

The Winners

an epilogue

What is the moral? Who rides may read.
When the night is thick and the tracks are blind
A friend at a pinch is a friend indeed,
But a fool to wait for the laggard behind.
Down to Gehenna or up to the Throne,
He travels the fastest who travels alone.

White hands cling to the tightened rein,
Slipping the spur from the booted heel,
Tenderest voices cry 'Turn again!'
Red lips tarnish the scabbarded steel.
High hopes faint on a warm hearth-stone –
He travels the fastest who travels alone.

One may fall but he falls by himself –
Falls by himself with himself to blame.
One may attain and to him is pelf –
Loot of the city in Gold or Fame.
Plunder of earth shall be all his own
Who travels the fastest and travels alone.

Wherefore the more ye be holpen and stayed,
Stayed by a friend in the hour of toil,
Sing the heretical song I have made –
His be the labour and yours be the spoil.
Win by his aid and the aid disown –
He travels the fastest who travels alone!

If

If you can keep your head when all about you
    Are losing theirs and blaming it on you,
If you can trust yourself when all men doubt you,
    But make allowance for their doubting too;
If you can wait and not be tired by waiting,
    Or being lied about, don't deal in lies,
Or being hated, don't give way to hating,
    And yet don't look too good, nor talk too wise:

If you can dream – and not make dreams your master;
    If you can think – and not make thoughts your aim;
If you can meet with Triumph and Disaster
    And treat those two imposters just the same;
If you can bear to hear the truth you've spoken
    Twisted by knaves to make a trap for fools,
Or watch the things you gave your life to, broken,
    And stoop and build 'em up with worn-out tools:

If you can make one heap of all your winnings
    And risk it on one turn of pitch-and-toss,
And lose, and start again at your beginnings
    And never breathe a word about your loss;
If you can force your heart and nerve and sinew
    To serve your turn long after they are gone,

And so hold on when there is nothing in you
    Except the Will which says to them: 'Hold on!'

If you can talk with crowds and keep your virtue,
    Or walk with Kings – nor lose the common touch,
If neither foes nor loving friends can hurt you,
    If all men count with you, but none too much;
If you can fill the unforgiving minute
    With sixty seconds' worth of distance run,
Yours is the Earth and everything that's in it,
    And – which is more – you'll be a Man, my son!

The Gods of the Copybook Headings

As I pass through my incarnations in every age and race,
I make my proper prostrations to the Gods of the Market-
    Place.
Peering through reverent fingers I watch them flourish and
    fall,
And the Gods of the Copybook Headings, I notice, outlast
    them all.

We were living in trees when they met us. They showed us
    each in turn
That Water would certainly wet us, as Fire would certainly
    burn:
But we found them lacking in Uplift, Vision and Breadth of
    Mind,
So we left them to teach the Gorillas while we followed the
    March of Mankind.

We moved as the Spirit listed. *They* never altered their pace,
Being neither cloud nor wind-borne like the Gods of the
    Market-Place;
But they always caught up with our progress, and presently
    word would come
That a tribe had been wiped off its icefield, or the lights had
    gone out in Rome.

With the Hopes that our World is built on they were utterly
    out of touch,
They denied that the Moon was Stilton; they denied she was
    even Dutch.
They denied that Wishes were Horses; they denied that a Pig
    had Wings.
So we worshipped the Gods of the Market Who promised
    these beautiful things.

When the Cambrian measures were forming, They promised
    perpetual peace.
They swore, if we gave them our weapons, that the wars of
    the tribes would cease.
But when we disarmed They sold us and delivered us bound
    to our foe,
And the Gods of the Copybook Headings said: '*Stick to the
    Devil you know.*'

On the first Feminian Sandstones we were promised the Fuller
    Life
(Which started by loving our neighbour and ended by loving
    his wife)
Till our women had no more children and the men lost
    reason and faith,
And the Gods of the Copybook Headings said: '*The Wages of
    Sin is Death.*'

In the Carboniferous Epoch we were promised abundance for
    all,
By robbing selected Peter to pay for collective Paul;
But, though we had plenty of money, there was nothing our
    money could buy,
And the Gods of the Copybook Headings said: '*If you don't
    work you die.*'

Then the Gods of the Market tumbled, and their smooth-
    tongued wizards withdrew,
And the hearts of the meanest were humbled and began to
    believe it was true
That All is not Gold that Glitters, and Two and Two make
    Four –

And the Gods of the Copybook Headings limped up to
    explain it once more.

★

As it will be in the future, it was at the birth of Man –
There are only four things certain since Social Progress
    began: –
That the Dog returns to his Vomit and the Sow returns to her
    Mire,
And the burnt Fool's bandaged finger goes wabbling back to
    the Fire;

And that after this is accomplished, and the brave new world
    begins
When all men are paid for existing and no man must pay for
    his sins,
As surely as Water will wet us, as surely as Fire will burn,
The Gods of the Copybook Headings with terror and
    slaughter return!

HILAIRE BELLOC

Ha'nacker Mill

Sally is gone that was so kindly
    Sally is gone from Ha'nacker Hill.
And the Briar grows ever since then so blindly
    And ever since then the clapper is still,
    And the sweeps have fallen from Ha'nacker Mill.

Ha'nacker Hill is in Desolation:
    Ruin a-top and a field unploughed.
And Spirits that call on a fallen nation
    Spirits that loved her calling aloud:
    Spirits abroad in a windy cloud.

Spirits that call and no one answers;
    Ha'nacker's down and England's done.
Wind and Thistle for pipe and dancers
    And never a ploughman under the Sun.
    Never a ploughman. Never a one.

JOHN McCREA

In Flanders Fields

In Flanders fields the poppies blow
Between the crosses, row on row
   That mark our place; and in the sky
   The larks, still bravely singing, fly
Scarce heard amid the guns below.

We are the Dead. Short days ago
We lived, felt dawn, saw sunset glow,
   Loved and were loved, and now we lie
      In Flanders fields.

Take up our quarrel with the foe:
To you from failing hands we throw
   The torch; be yours to hold it high.
   If ye break faith with us who die
We shall not sleep, though poppies grow
      In Flanders fields.

G. K. CHESTERTON

The Donkey

When fishes flew and forests walked
   And figs grew upon thorn,
Some moment when the moon was blood
   Then surely I was born.

With monstrous head and sickening cry
   And ears like errant wings,
The devil's walking parody
   On all four-footed things.

The tattered outlaw of the earth,
   Of ancient crooked will;
Starve, scourge, deride me: I am dumb,
   I keep my secret still.

Fools! For I also had my hour;
    One far fierce hour and sweet:
There was a shout about my ears,
    And palms before my feet.

Elegy in a Country Churchyard

The men that worked for England
They have their graves at home:
And bees and birds of England
About the cross can roam.

But they that fought for England,
Following a falling star,
Alas, alas for England
They have their graves afar.

And they that rule in England,
In stately conclave met,
Alas, alas for England
They have no graves as yet.

Lepanto

White founts falling in the courts of the sun,
And the Soldan of Byzantium is smiling as they run;
There is laughter like the fountains in that face of all men
    feared,
It stirs the forest darkness, the darkness of his beard,
It curls the blood-red crescent, the crescent of his lips,
For the inmost sea of all the earth is shaken with his ships.
They have dared the white republics up the capes of Italy,
They have dashed the Adriatic round the Lion of the Sea,
And the Pope has cast his arms abroad for agony and loss,
And called the kings of Christendom for swords about the
    Cross,
The cold queen of England is looking in the glass;

The shadow of the Valois is yawning at the Mass;
From evening isles fantastical rings faint the Spanish gun,
And the Lord upon the Golden Horn is laughing in the sun.

Dim drums throbbing, in the hills half heard,
Where only on a nameless throne a crownless prince has stirred,
Where, risen from a doubtful seat and half-attainted stall,
The last knight of Europe takes weapons from the wall,
The last and lingering troubadour to whom the bird has sung,
That once went singing southward when all the world was
      young,
In that enormous silence, tiny and unafraid,
Comes up along a winding road the noise of the Crusade.
Strong gongs groaning as the guns boom far,
Don John of Austria is going to the war,
Stiff flags straining in the night-blasts cold
In the gloom black-purple, in the glint old-gold,
Torchlight crimson on the copper kettle-drums,
Then the tuckets, then the trumpets, then the cannon, and he
      comes.
Don John laughing in the brave beard curled,
Spurning of his stirrups like the thrones of all the world,
Holding his head up for a flag of all the free.
Love-light of Spain – hurrah!
Death-light of Africa!
Don John of Austria
Is riding to the sea.

Mahound is in his paradise above the evening star,
(*Don John of Austria is going to the war.*)
He moves a mighty turban on the timeless houri's knees,
His turban that is woven of the sunset and the seas.
He shakes the peacock gardens as he rises from his ease,
And he strides among the tree-tops and is taller than the trees,
And his voice through all the garden is a thunder sent to bring
Black Azrael and Ariel and Ammon on the wing.
Giants and the Genii,
Multiplex of wing and eye,
Whose strong obedience broke the sky
When Solomon was king.

They rush in red and purple from the red clouds of the morn,
From temples where the yellow gods shut up their eyes in
      scorn;
They rise in green robes roaring from the green hells of the sea
Where fallen skies and evil hues and eyeless creatures be;
On them the sea-valves cluster and the grey sea-forests curl,
Splashed with a splendid sickness, the sickness of the pearl;
They swell in sapphire smoke out of the blue cracks of the
      ground, –
They gather and they wonder and give worship to Mahound.
And he saith, 'Break up the mountains where the hermit-folk
      may hide,
And sift the red and silver sands lest bone of saint abide,
And chase the Giaours flying night and day, not giving rest,
For that which was our trouble comes again out of the west.
We have set the seal of Solomon on all things under sun,
Of knowledge and of sorrow and endurance of things done,
But a noise is in the mountains, in the mountains, and I know
The voice that shook our palaces – four hundred years ago:
It is he that saith not 'Kismet'; it is he that knows not Fate;
It is Richard, it is Raymond, it is Godfrey in the gate!
It is he whose loss is laughter when he counts the wager worth,
Put down your feet upon him, that our peace be on the earth.'
For he heard drums groaning and he heard guns jar,
(*Don John of Austria is going to the war.*)
Sudden and still – hurrah!
Bolt from Iberia!
Don John of Austria
Is gone by Alcalar.

St. Michael's on his Mountain in the sea-roads of the north
(*Don John of Austria is girt and going forth.*)
Where the grey seas glitter and the sharp tides shift
And the sea folk labour and the red sails lift.
He shakes his lance of iron and he claps his wings of stone;
The noise is gone through Normandy; the noise is gone alone;
The North is full of tangled things and texts and aching eyes
And dead is all the innocence of anger and surprise,
And Christian killeth Christian in a narrow dusty room,
And Christian dreadeth Christ that hath a newer face of doom,
And Christian hateth Mary that God kissed in Galilee,

But Don John of Austria is riding to the sea.
Don John calling through the blast and the eclipse
Crying with the trumpet, with the trumpet of his lips,
Trumpet that sayeth ha!
Domino gloria!
Don John of Austria
Is shouting to the ships.

King Philip's in his closet with the Fleece about his neck
(*Don John of Austria is armed upon the deck.*)
The walls are hung with velvet that is black and soft as sin,
And little dwarfs creep out of it and little dwarfs creep in.
He holds a crystal phial that has colours like the moon,
He touches, and it tingles, and he trembles very soon,
And his face is as a fungus of a leprous white and grey
Like plants in the high houses that are shuttered from the day,
And death is in the phial, and the end of noble work,
But Don John of Austria has fired upon the Turk.
Don John's hunting, and his hounds have bayed –
Booms away past Italy the rumour of his raid.
Gun upon gun, ha! ha!
Gun upon gun, hurrah!
Don John of Austria
Has loosed the cannonade.

The Pope was in his chapel before day or battle broke,
(*Don John of Austria is hidden in the smoke.*)
The hidden room in a man's house where God sits all the year,
The secret window whence the world looks small and very
    dear.
He sees as in a mirror on the monstrous twilight sea
The crescent of his cruel ships whose name is mystery;
They fling great shadows foe-wards, making Cross and Castle
    dark,
They veil the plumèd lions on the galleys of St. Mark;
And above the ships are palaces of brown, black-bearded chiefs,
And below the ships are prisons, where the multitudinous
    griefs,
Christian captives sick and sunless, all a labouring race repines
Like a race in sunken cities, like a nation in the mines.

They are lost like slaves that swat, and in the skies of morning
     hung
The stairways of the tallest gods when tyranny was young.
They are countless, voiceless, hopeless as those fallen or fleeing
     on
Before the high Kings' horses in the granite of Babylon.
And many a one grows witless in his quiet room in hell
Where a yellow face looks inward through the lattice of his
     cell,
And he finds his God forgotten, and he seeks no more a sign –
(But Don John of Austria has burst the battle-line!)
Don John pounding from the slaughter-painted poop,
Purpling all the ocean like a bloody pirate's sloop,
Scarlet running over on the silvers and the golds,
Breaking of the hatches up and bursting of the holds,
Thronging of the thousands up that labour under sea
White for bliss and blind for sun and stunned for liberty.
Vivat Hispania!
Domino Gloria!
Don John of Austria
Has set his people free!

Cervantes on his galley sets the sword back in the sheath
(Don John of Austria rides homeward with a wreath.)
And he sees across a weary land a straggling road in Spain,
Up which a lean and foolish knight forever rides in vain,
And he smiles, but not as Sultans smile, and settles back the
     blade . . .
(But Don John of Austria rides home from the Crusade.)

The Secret People

Smile at us, pay us, pass us; but do not quite forget,
For we are the people of England, that never has spoken yet.
There is many a fat farmer that drinks less cheerfully,
There is many a free French peasant who is richer and sadder
     than we.
There are no folk in the whole world so helpless or so wise.
There is hunger in our bellies, there is laughter in our eyes;

You laugh at us and love us, both mugs and eyes are wet:
Only you do not know us. For we have not spoken yet.

The fine French kings came over in a flutter of flags and
    dames.
We liked their smiles and battles, but we never could say their
    names.
The blood ran red to Bosworth and the high French lords
    went down;
There was naught but a naked people under a naked crown.
And the eyes of the King's Servants turned terribly every way,
And the gold of the King's Servants rose higher every day.
They burnt the homes of the shaven men, that had been
    quaint and kind,
Till there was no bed in a monk's house, nor food that man
    could find.
The inns of God where no man paid, that were the wall of the
    weak,
The King's Servants ate them all. And still we did not speak.

And the face of the King's Servants grew greater than the
    King:
He tricked them, and they trapped him, and stood round him
    in a ring.
The new grave lords closed round him, that had eaten the
    abbey's fruits,
And the men of the new religion, with their Bibles in their
    boots,
We saw their shoulders moving, to menace or discuss,
And some were pure and some were vile; but none took heed
    of us.
We saw the King as they killed him, and his face was proud
    and pale;
And a few men talked of freedom, while England talked of ale.

A war that we understood not came over the world and woke
Americans, Frenchmen, Irish; but we knew not the things
    they spoke.
They talked about rights and nature and peace and the people's
    reign:

238

And the squires, our masters, bade us fight; and never scorned
  us again.
Weak if we be for ever, could none condemn us then;
Men called us serfs and drudges; men knew that we were men.
In foam and flame at Trafalgar, on Albuera plains,
We did and died like lions, to keep ourselves in chains,
We lay in living ruins; firing and fearing not
The strange fierce face of the Frenchman who knew for what
  they fought,
And the man who seemed to be more than man we strained
  against and broke;
And we broke our own rights with him. And still we never
  spoke.

Our patch of glory ended; we never heard guns again.
But the squire seemed struck in the saddle; he was foolish, as if
  in pain
He leaned on a staggering lawyer, he clutched a cringing Jew,
He was stricken; it may be, after all, he was stricken at
  Waterloo.
Or perhaps the shades of the shaven men, whose spoil is in his
  house,
Come back in shining shapes at last to spoil his last carouse:
We only know the last sad squires ride slowly towards the
  sea,
And a new people takes the land: and still it is not we.

They have given us into the hands of the new unhappy lords,
Lords without anger and honour, who dare not carry their
  swords.
They fight by shuffling papers; they have bright dead alien
  eyes;
They look at our labour and laughter as a tired man looks at
  flies.
And the load of their loveless pity is worse than the ancient
  wrongs,
Their doors are shut in the evening; and they know no songs.

We hear men speaking for us of new laws strong and sweet,
Yet is there no man speaketh as we speak in the street.
It may be we shall rise the last as Frenchmen rose the first,

Our wrath come after Russia's wrath and our wrath be the
    worst.
It may be we are meant to mark with our riot and our rest
God's scorn for all men governing. It may be beer is best.
But we are the people of England; and we have not spoken
    yet.
Smile at us, pay us, pass us. But do not quite forget.

JOHN MASEFIELD

Cargoes

Quinquireme of Nineveh from distant Ophir
Rowing home to haven in sunny Palestine,
With a cargo of ivory,
And apes and peacocks,
Sandalwood, cedarwood, and sweet white wine.

Stately Spanish galleon coming from the Isthmus,
Dipping through the Tropics by the palm-green shores,
With a cargo of diamonds,
Emeralds, amethysts,
Topazes, and cinnamon, and gold moidores.

Dirty British coaster with a salt-caked smoke stack
Butting through the Channel in the mad March days,
With a cargo of Tyne coal,
Road-rail, pig-lead,
Firewood, iron-ware, and cheap tin trays.

Sea-Fever

I must go down to the seas again, to the lonely sea and the
    sky,
And all I ask is a tall ship and a star to steer her by,
And the wheel's kick and the wind's song and the white sails
    shaking,
And a grey mist on the sea's face and a grey dawn breaking.

I must go down to the seas again, for the call of the running
   tide
Is a wild call and a clear call that may not be denied;
And all I ask is a windy day with the white clouds flying,
And the flung spray and the blown spume, and the sea-gulls
   crying.

I must go down to the seas again, to the vagrant gypsy life,
To the gull's way and the whale's way where the wind's like
   a whetted knife;
And all I ask is a merry yarn from a laughing fellow-rover,
And quiet sleep and a sweet dream when the long trick's over.

JAMES ELROY FLECKER

The Golden Journey to Samarkand

Prologue

We who with songs beguile your pilgrimage
   And swear that Beauty lives though lilies die,
We Poets of the proud old lineage
   Who sing to find your hearts, we know not why, –

What shall we tell you? Tales, marvellous tales
   Of ships and stars and isles where good men rest,
Where nevermore the rose of sunset pales,
   And winds and shadows fall toward the West:

And there the world's first huge white-bearded kings
   In dim glades sleeping, murmur in their sleep,
And closer round their breasts the ivy clings,
   Cutting its pathway slow and red and deep.

II

And how beguile you? Death has no repose
   Warmer and deeper than that Orient sand
Which hides the beauty and bright faith of those
   Who made the Golden Journey to Samarkand.

And now they wait and whiten peaceably,
   Those conquerors, those poets, those so fair:

241

They know time comes, not only you and I,
    But the whole world shall whiten, here or there;

When those long caravans that cross the plain
    With dauntless feet and sound of silver bells
Put forth no more for glory or for gain,
    Take no more solace from the palm-girt wells.

When the great markets by the sea shut fast
    All that calm Sunday that goes on and on:
When even lovers find their peace at last,
    And Earth is but a star, that once had shone.

RUPERT BROOKE

The Soldier

If I should die, think only this of me:
    That there's some corner of a foreign field
That is for ever England. There shall be
    In that rich earth a richer dust concealed;
A dust whom England bore, shaped, made aware,
    Gave, once, her flowers to love, her ways to roam,
A body of England's, breathing English air,
    Washed by the rivers, blest by suns of home.

And think, this heart, all evil shed away,
    A pulse in the eternal mind, no less
        Gives somewhere back the thoughts by England given;
Her sights and sounds; dreams happy as her day;
    And laughter, learnt of friends; and gentleness,
        In hearts at peace, under an English heaven.

ALAN SEEGER

Rendezvous

I have a rendezvous with Death
    At some disputed barricade,
    When Spring comes back with rustling shade

And apple-blossoms fill the air –
I have a rendezvous with Death
When Spring brings back blue days and fair.

It may be he shall take my hand
And lead me into his dark land
And close my eyes and quench my breath –
It may be I shall pass him still.
I have a rendezvous with Death
On some scarred slope of battered hill,
When Spring comes round again this year
And the first meadow-flowers appear.

God knows 'twere better to be deep
Pillowed in silk and scented down,
Where love throbs out in blissful sleep,
Pulse nigh to pulse, and breath to breath,
Where hushed awakenings are dear . . .
But I've a rendezvous with Death
At midnight in some flaming town,
When Spring trips north again this year,
And I to my pledged word am true,
I shall not fail that rendezvous.

JULIAN GRENFELL

Into Battle

The naked earth is warm with Spring,
  And with green grass and bursting trees
Leans to the sun's gaze glorying,
  And quivers in the sunny breeze;

And life is colour and warmth and light,
  And a striving evermore for these;
And he is dead who will not fight;
  And who dies fighting has increase.

The fighting man shall from the sun
  Take warmth, and life from the glowing earth;

Speed with the light-foot winds to run,
  And with the trees to newer birth;
And find, when fighting shall be done,
  Great rest, and fullness after dearth.

All the bright company of Heaven
  Hold him in their high comradeship,
The Dog-Star, and the Sisters Seven,
  Orion's Belt and sworded hip.

The woodland trees that stand together,
  They stand to him each one a friend;
They gently speak in the windy weather;
  They guide to valley and ridge's end.

The kestrel hovering by day,
  And the little owls that call by night,
Bid him be swift and keen as they,
  As keen of ear, as swift of sight.

The blackbird sings to him, 'Brother, brother,
  If this be the last song you shall sing,
Sing well, for you may not sing another;
  Brother, sing.'

In dreary, doubtful waiting hours,
  Before the brazen frenzy starts,
The horses show him nobler powers;
  O patient eyes, courageous hearts!

And when the burning moment breaks,
  And all things else are out of mind,
And only joy of battle takes
  Him by the throat, and makes him blind,

Through joy and blindness he shall know,
  Not caring much to know, that still
Nor lead nor steel shall reach him, so
  That it be not the Destined Will.

The thundering line of battle stands,
   And in the air Death moans and sings;
But Day shall clasp him with strong hands,
   And Night shall fold him in soft wings.

ACKNOWLEDGEMENTS

Permission to use copyright material is gratefully acknowledged to the following: A. D. Peters & Co. Ltd. for 'Ha'nacker Mill' by Hilaire Belloc; Miss Dorothy Collins and A. P. Watt & Son for 'The Donkey', 'Elegy in a Country Churchyard', 'Lepanto', and The Secret People' by G. K. Chesterton; the Society of Authors for the Estate of A. E. Housman and Jonathan Cape Ltd. for '1887' and 'The Recruit' from the *Collected Poems* by A. E. Housman; the National Trust and the Macmillan Co. of London & Basingstoke for 'If', 'The Winners', and 'The Gods of the Copy-book Headings' from *The Definitive Edition of Rudyard Kipling's Verse*; the National Trust and Methuen & Co. Ltd. for 'Boots', 'For All We Have and Are', 'Recessional', 'Tommy', 'The Ballad of East and West', and 'Danny Deever' from *The Definitive Edition of Rudyard Kipling's Verse*; the Society of Authors for the Estate of John Masefield for 'Cargoes' and 'Sea-Fever' by John Masefield; Mr. Peter Newbolt for 'Admirals All', 'Ireland, Ireland', 'Drake's Drum', 'He Fell among Thieves', and 'Vitaï Lampada' from *Poems: New and Old* by Sir Henry Newbolt; Mrs. Sonia Brownell Orwell and Secker & Warburg Ltd. for the quotation from *The Collected Essays, Journalism and Letters of George Orwell*, ed. Sonia Orwell and Ian Angus, Vol. II, pp. 195–6; Mr. M. B. Yeats, Miss Anne Yeats and the Macmillan Co. of London & Basingstoke for 'Easter 1916' and 'The Lake Isle of Innisfree' from *The Collected Poems of W. B. Yeats*.

INDEX OF FIRST LINES

INDEX OF POETS